Grimgar of Fantasy an

level.12 - That Was the Beginning of a Legend
Revolving Around a Certain Island and Dragons

Written by: **Ao Jyumonji**
Illustrations by: **Eiri Shirai**

The setting sun was poking its face out from beyond the edge of the sea, illuminating the surface of the water.

"Splooooosh!"

Life is full of ups and downs, mountains and valleys.
Uh, actually, it's just mountains lately, I guess.
Really, there's been a lot that's happened.

Still, we're alive, Manato, Moguzo.

Grimgar
of
Fantasy
and
Ash

GRIMGAR OF FANTASY AND ASH, LEVEL. 12

First published in Japan in 2018 by
OVERLAP Inc., Ltd., Tokyo.
English translation rights arranged with
OVERLAP Inc., Ltd., Tokyo.

Follow Seven Seas Entertainment online at
sevenseasentertainment.com.
Experience J-Novel Club books online at j-novel.club.

TRANSLATION: Sean McCann
J-NOVEL EDITOR: Emily Sorensen
COVER DESIGN: KC Fabellon
INTERIOR LAYOUT & DESIGN: Clay Gardner
PREPRESS TECHNICIAN: Rhiannon Rasmussen-Silverstein
COPY EDITOR: Brian Kearney
PROOFREADER: Christina Lynn
LIGHT NOVEL EDITOR: Nibedita Sen
MANAGING EDITOR: Julie Davis
ASSOCIATE PUBLISHER: Adam Arnold
PUBLISHER: Jason DeAngelis

ISBN: 978-1-64505-212-8
Printed in Canada
First Printing: March 2020
10 9 8 7 6 5 4 3 2 1

Grimgar of Fantasy and Ash

level. 12 — That Was the Beginning of a Legend Revolving Around a Certain Island and Dragons

Presented by
AO JYUMONJI

Illustrated by
EIRI SHIRAI

Seven Seas

novel club

Table of Contents

Grimgar
of
Fantasy *and* Ash

1 | We Ended Up in a Hole Somehow

"...U RGH." Haruhiro covered his face with the hand in which he held his stiletto with a backhand grip.

There was some sort of swarm of small creatures flying toward him. Bats? No. Bugs, maybe?

In front of Haruhiro, Kuzaku started to make a fuss, swinging around the lamp he was carrying. "Wh-wh-wh-whooooooaaaaaaa, i-i-i-i-isn't this really bad?!"

The light swayed violently. There was the unceasing sound of little creatures hitting the lamp.

"Sheesh! What's goin' on?" Yume shouted from the back.

"—be eaten?!" Shihoru asked, her first words muffled and leaving room for multiple interpretations.

Immediately, Merry replied, "They can't be eaten!" apparently having taken the interpretation that it was a question about whether or not they were edible.

Without missing a beat, Setora asked, "You know that?!"

Merry didn't answer. She probably didn't have time to. That was how Haruhiro interpreted it.

Kiichi the gray nyaa let out a frightening yowl.

"I-It's fine. It'll be fine...probably." Lowering his posture, Haruhiro offered reassurances that were like uncertainty incarnate, and tried to ascertain the nature of the little creatures.

It really looked like they were bats that lived in the depths of this cave—no, not a cave, it was an artificial hole—and when Haruhiro and the others entered, they were surprised and came out.

But they were a bit like cockroaches, too. Whatever they were, he had the sense, somehow, that they weren't all that dangerous. Having been through hell more times than he'd have liked, his body responded to that sort of danger instantly most of the time.

This had to be fine...

Probably.

For what felt like forty-five seconds, he stayed put. The swarm of little creatures seemed to have flown off, for the most part. Only for the most part, though. Not all of them. There were still one or two beating their wings and flying around.

"They're like something halfway between a beetle and a flying squirrel..." Kuzaku muttered.

Oh, I see, thought Haruhiro. *That's another way to put it.*

A cross between a beetle and a flying squirrel gave off a better impression than a cross between a bat and a cockroach. Kuzaku was the type to see the good side of things, which was the opposite of Haruhiro. That was a matter of inclination, though, so even if Haruhiro wanted to change it, he couldn't.

"Looks like it's fine now, so let's move on," Haruhiro said.

"Sounds good," Kuzaku nodded.

"Ah!" Yume raised her voice. "One of them critters, it's gone and clung to Shihoru's back."

"Eek...?! Y-you're kidding! G-g-g-get it off, please..."

"Don't make a fuss over something so little," Setora chided her. Then she tore the little creature from Shihoru's back, threw it to the ground, and stomped on it. "There."

Seeing that, Yume let out a little cry of "Nooo!" and covered her face with her hands. "There wasn't any need to go and step on it, y'know. You could've let it go..."

"There's one on your leg, too, hunter."

"Yikes! Meow, get it off! Ahh!"

"...You just stomped on it real hard there," Setora said dryly. "Weren't you going to let it go?"

"Meh. Come on, that critter, it was about to bite Yume, y'know?"

"They suck blood, so be careful," Merry said suddenly. "Not too much, though, I don't think. But if they're diseased, I can't guarantee we won't catch whatever they have."

Everyone went silent.

Yeah. Well, who wouldn't?

That information sounded pretty important to Haruhiro, and he felt like maybe it would have been nice if she had shared it a bit sooner. However, saying that would require confronting his doubts about why Merry knew, and so, though he wanted to ask, it was too hard for him to do it.

Stuff like this happened occasionally. When, as a result, he ended up feeling awkward, he might or might not have found himself wishing they had someone like that idiot who used to be in the group, who was willing to bluntly say the things that were hard to say.

"Aren't we going?" Setora, one of the ones in this group with less social grace, spoke up.

That saved him. Haruhiro and the rest moved on.

The hole was about two meters across, and a little over two meters high. Kuzaku, being as tall as he was, was bent over a bit. Incidentally, the hole had been far narrower and lower at the entrance. Both of the walls and the floor were covered in moss or lichen, and there were mysterious mushroom-like or fern-like plants growing, and what seemed to be the dung of animals of some sort piled up, but it was nearly flat.

This hole didn't go straight, either. It would go down, and then turn.

"There's something here." Kuzaku came to a stop, tapping his hand on the right wall.

He brought the lamp closer. It looked like there was something resembling a door there.

Haruhiro moved up and investigated. It was, indeed, a door. Not made of wood. Or of metal. It was a stone door. Even the handles and keyhole were made of stone.

Haruhiro was a thief, even if he wasn't a great one. He could at least tell that this was an unusual door. It wasn't ostentatious in the slightest, but its entire surface was smooth, and of careful construction.

"Wow, dwarves are awesome..." Haruhiro got out his thieving tools and started Picking. Carefully probing the inside of the lock, he came to understand its design. If he tried to unlock it, it wouldn't be impossible for it to spring a trap, so he had to be cautious. Though, if the lock was metal, it might have rusted to the point he couldn't do anything with it.

Well, it took some time, but he managed to unlock it somehow.

"It's not locked anymore, but getting it open is still going to be a pain," he said. "It's made of stone and pretty heavy, after all."

"Me, I'll do it. Haruhiro, you get back." Kuzaku started to force open the stone door.

Setora muttered something about, "Pure idiot-strength..."

"I'm built for this stuff. It's my one strong suit," Kuzaku said with a smile.

Beyond the door was a four-meter-square room. There were shelves installed in it, and two large boxes left in the corners. These were also of stone construction.

The equipment left out on the shelves was badly rusted, and it wouldn't be of any use in its current state.

The issue was what was in the boxes that were close to one meter tall and wide, with a depth of about eighty centimeters. Haruhiro closely inspected them.

"I don't see any locks, and no traps that'd spring upon opening them...I think, but honestly I can't be that confident. Most likely, I can't lift up the lids myself. I'm sure a dwarf could manage it easy, though."

"That's my cue, huh?" Kuzaku passed the lamp to Yume and went to put his hands on the lid.

Haruhiro hurriedly stopped him. "No, listen, I'm telling you I don't know if it's safe or not."

"It doesn't seem trapped, right? As far as you can see."

"Only as far as I can see, though. Even if it's not trapped, there could be something weird inside."

"How do you feel about it, Haruhiro? In your gut, I mean."

"Hmm. I dunno if my gut can be trusted here to begin with..."

"I trust it. If you think we're good to go, I'm gonna go ahead and do it. If you say to stop, I'll do that. Oh, and if something bad happens, I won't have any regrets, okay?"

Yume nodded. "That's love, all right," she said, though it was total nonsense.

That made Shihoru burst out laughing, choking and spluttering, and then Merry cleared her throat loudly for some reason.

"Love?" Setora tilted her head to the side. The gray nyaa Kiichi was fondly rubbing his face against her feet. "Paladin, are you what they would call a homosexual?"

"Nah, I like Haruhiro, but not that way. I dunno. Basically, I trust him."

"I'm amazed that you can say that so unabashedly."

"Huh? Is it embarrassing? Ohh. Maybe? I might be starting to feel a bit embarrassed now. But it's how I really feel. I don't want to lie, you know, and I don't tend to. Well, shucks."

Haruhiro was starting to get embarrassed himself, so he wished Kuzaku would stop it.

When Kuzaku said, "Aww, damn, this is really embarrassing. Whatever. I'm opening it!" then threw open the stone lid, Haruhiro wished he could've stopped this too.

"Ah! Kuzaku, wai—"

"Whoa! Sorry, Haruhiro, but it looks like nothing happened?"

In the box were a number of short swords, a shield, a helmet, and a small number of accessories. They were practically like new. From the look of them, they were good quality, too. The dwarves must have poured their souls into making these.

It looked like Kuzaku could use the shield and helmet. The swords included a broad, heavy knife and a short sword, two daggers, and a strange knife with a wavy flame-like blade. The women could put on the accessories if they wanted to, and they could sell the rest. The question of where they'd sell them, and who would buy them, could be set aside for now. Thinking about it would just make things harder.

Setora took the short sword and a normal dagger, while Haruhiro took the other dagger and the weird knife with the flame-like blade.

Truthfully, the stiletto he was so used to holding in his dominant right hand, as well as the knife with the hand guard he used in his left, were damaged to the point where a little sharpening wasn't going to be enough. It was a shame to do it, but he decided to throw them away in the name of keeping things light.

For convenience's sake, he named the dagger with the fire-like blade the flame dagger. Kuzaku could carry the wide, heavy dagger as a backup weapon.

Other than that, there were spear tips and ax heads inside the box. If they attached shafts to them, they could likely be used as spears or axes, but they were bulky, so they'd have to leave them behind.

"It's a double harvest," Yume grinned. "This went divingly."

"I think you mean a rich harvest, not a double one," Haruhiro said. "How about a haul instead? Also, it's swimmingly, not divingly..."

While driven by a sense of duty to correct the way Yume talked, he saw Kuzaku about to open the second box out of the corner of his eye.

"Whuh..." He was at a loss for words.

"Huh?" Kuzaku opened the lid, then turned to look at Haruhiro. "Is something up? Oh..."

"Now, listen, don't just open it up because that feels like the thing to do..."

"Something's—" Merry looked up to the ceiling.

Noise.

There was a low sound.

"Out of here, hurry!" Haruhiro shouted.

Yume practically dragged Shihoru as she flew out of the room. Merry, Setora, and Kiichi followed. Haruhiro whacked Kuzaku on the back.

"Come on, hurry!"

"Haruhiro, I'll be fine! Go on ahead!"

"Listen, we don't need to take turns! Come on already, we don't have time for—Oh, crap!"

The noise got louder. The whole room was trembling. The ceiling. The ceiling was coming down. Was that the kind of trap it was?

"Wahhhhhh!"

Haruhiro and Kuzaku rolled out of the room in unison. Immediately afterwards, the room came down all at once.

"That was close! We nearly got crushed!" Kuzaku cried.

"Kuzaku, it's because you recklessly opened that box. This happened because you weren't cautious..."

"Hey, hey, Haru-kun, it's still kinda weird, y'know? Like it's rumble, rumble, rumblin'."

"Huh?! It's rumble, rumble, rumblin'...?" Haruhiro was talkin' like Yume despite himself.

That ain't the way I talk, he thought to himself. *"Ain't" isn't something I say, either.*

"From deeper in...?" Merry furrowed her brow.

That was right. This cave—no—this dwarven mine, this dwarf hole, which was like a natural hole that the dwarves had reworked to suit their needs, still went deeper. There were likely rooms other than the one they'd just been in, and there might be yet more treasure waiting inside. However, like Yume said, there was an ominous rumbling coming from those depths. There was definitely something coming. Was it something big?

"Run!" Haruhiro shouted.

It was heartbreaking, but they'd have to give up on the treasure.

Haruhiro sent his comrades on ahead, while he stayed behind.

Kuzaku was shouting his name or something, but he just thought, *It's fine, you get going already. This isn't the time to worry about other people. Run as fast as you can. Yeah, it's definitely further in. It's coming from inside. It's like, I dunno, a mass of rock? Like a huge rock ball is going to come rolling? I feel like I've seen that somewhere, or maybe I haven't, but whatever. If we don't run, it's going to crush us flat.*

Naturally, Haruhiro ran, too, bringing up the rear.

How close was the rock ball? Was there really a rock ball to begin with? Was it something else, maybe?

Even if he turned back, it was pitch black, so he couldn't see.

It felt like the sound was getting closer. Yeah, that would make him feel rushed. If he were to claim otherwise, he'd be lying.

That said, Haruhiro still had a little bit of his composure. But he couldn't run any faster. Shihoru was in front of him, after all. He couldn't exactly pass her.

What was he going to do now?

It was a quandary.

2 | The Flames Waver with Hesitation

THIS AREA NOW CALLED THE FRONTIER had once been made up of human kingdoms with names like Arabakia, Nananka, and Ishmal.

The elves, dwarves, and gnomes had prospered as a result of fostering cordial relations with the human race. But the orcs, kobolds, goblins, and others were still driven out, persecuted, alienated, and thoroughly despised.

For the orcs, in particular, it wasn't just their bodies and physical abilities. Their intellect was in no way inferior to that of the humans, either. However, humans had built nations before the orcs, and spread out across the fertile land.

Even when the orcs, driven by humans into inferior lands like the Nehi Desert, the Plateau of Falling Ash, and the Plains of Mold, had united into tribes based on blood relations, it was all they could do to survive.

Around a hundred and fifty years ago, one calling himself the No-Life King had appeared, changing everything.

Giving birth to the undead and expanding his power in short order had placed pressure on the human kingdoms. In addition, he had encouraged unity between the various orcish tribes, and set up a kingdom for them.

Before that, the humans had seen the orcs as no more than a savage race, more akin to beasts, and had looked down on them. However, once the orcs gained a king, they established the systems of a state rapidly, and, arming themselves, they began to invade the human realms.

Forming a pact with the orcs, kobolds, goblins, and the gray elves who'd broken away from the other elves, the No-Life King established the Alliance of Kings, and boldly declared war against the kingdoms of the human race.

The human kingdoms of Ishmal and Nananka were destroyed, and the Kingdom of Arabakia fled to the south of the Tenryu Mountains.

Elves, dwarves, and gnomes were also caught in the bloody chaos of war. The elves relied on the natural barrier presented by the Shadow Forest, primarily fighting in self-defense, but the dwarves swung their swords and axes with a daring and resolution greater than that of any human, putting up a fierce battle.

The famed dwarven Steel Axe Corps faced an overwhelmingly larger force from the Alliance of Kings at the Bordo Plains, never retreating as they put up a hard fight, but they were wiped out.

The elves of the Shadow Forest were supposed to send rein-forcements to help the Steel Axe Corps, but they were blocked by a detached force from the Alliance of Kings, and were unable to fulfill their promise.

All of that aside, in the midst of the intense fighting, the dwarves dug shelters here and there, storing weapons, armor, supplies, and rations in them.

These shelters, called dwarf holes, offered a place for the defeated dwarven soldiers to flee to, as well as bases to launch a counteroffensive from.

During their journey east towards the sea, Haruhiro and the others had, coincidentally, found one such dwarf hole.

Haruhiro and the others had been able to gain a number of the treasures the dwarves had tucked away there over a hundred years ago, but now had fallen for a dwarven trap.

It wasn't easy to survive those.

"I'm seriously sorry about this." Kuzaku was performing a kowtow.

Haruhiro fed a branch into the fire, thinking, *With a kowtow like that, you've got a long way to go before you're up to the level of the legendary kowtow master. Maybe it's better if you never do get to that level. I wonder if that legendary kowtow master is still alive and well someplace. Well, dead or alive, it's none of my con-cern. Anyway, this fire's kind of nice. Though we're at a pretty high altitude, it's summer, so it's not cold at all. But a fire is still nice. It's relaxing.*

"Well, yeah..." Yume climbed a nearby tree, dangling her legs from a branch, and looking around the area. It looked like she was relaxing and taking it easy, but she was actually proactively taking it upon herself to be a lookout. "Fortunately, nothing much ended up gettin' lost. No one was hurt at all, either, so it went well, that's what Yume thinks."

"Nah..." Kuzaku raised his face a little. "That's only something you can say in hindsight. I think I really do need to reflect on my actions. Make things proper."

"Were you in a bit of an odd frame of mind?" Shihoru asked, nestling close to Merry by the fire.

Kuzaku hung his head again, groaning in thought. Then, after a short while, he raised his face again.

"Maybe? Like, 'Oh, crap, it's a dwarf hole! Maybe there are some super awesome weapons and stuff here!' It was the first adventure-y thing we'd done in a while. I may have been excited..."

"Are you a child?" Setora spat as she checked on the pot cooking over the fire.

"...I'm a kid. 'Kay. Sorry."

"Even though you're bigger than any of us."

"...Sure am. Whew. 'Kay. I'm not sure what to say."

"For a start, paladin, what is with the way you're talking?"

"Oh, the way I'm kind of polite? That's what I'm aiming for, at least."

"You're not polite in the least. It almost feels like you're mocking me."

"You're misunderstanding. 'Kay. Oops, did it again. Is this becoming a habit...?"

Kuzaku had gotten out of kowtow mode at some point, and he was now kneeling and scratching the back of his head.

What was Merry thinking as she looked into the crackling flames? She might have just been zoning out, but Haruhiro couldn't help but imagine all sorts of things that might be running through Merry's head.

It wasn't good to do that. He shouldn't just make things up; he needed to talk to her and ask. Merry was right in front of his eyes, after all. That was certainly true, but...

"Haruhiro-kun?" Shihoru called out, bringing Haruhiro back to his senses.

"Uh, sure. What is it?"

"I don't think it's right to ignore Kuzaku when he's apologizing..." she complained.

Haruhiro lowered his eyes. "Erm..." He rubbed his nose. "I didn't mean to ignore him, though..."

"I don't mind. It happens a lot with Haruhiro."

"Huh? I ignore people?"

"I usually decide to take it as, 'Ohh, he's mad. Uh-oh. I'd better think about what I did.'"

"Oh, yeah? So I do that... I never realized. Sorry. Ignoring people's not good. If no one says anything, it's hard to notice you're doing it, I guess. Thanks, Shihoru. I'll be careful not to."

"No, I should apologize," she said. "I may have been butting in when it wasn't my business."

"Not at all. I'm grateful that you told me. Hold on... Kuzaku, what're you grinning for?"

"Grinning? Was I? Well, you know how it is. I'm just glad we have you as leader."

"You're doing a swell job of creeping me out when you say stuff like that..."

"No way. It was creepy? Uh-oh. I tend to say whatever comes into my head, y'know?"

"What a loyal dog you are," Setora snorted, removing the pot from the fire.

The skewers lined up around the fire were nice and crisp. Setora pulled one out of the ground, sticking a piece of meat into her mouth. She chewed, then nodded.

"Let's eat. Hey, hunter, you come down here, too. Kiichi is looking around, so it's fine."

Everyone gathered around the fire, eating Setora's snail and mushroom soup along with the skewers of venison. The ingredients, including snails, venison, various herbs, and variety of mushrooms, had been gathered by Yume, Kiichi, and Setora.

When they bit into the skewers seasoned with herbs, juice poured out, and it was simple but delicious. The soup had the deer's organs in it, too, providing a thick broth. Even so, the herbs added a slight mugwort-like taste, refreshing like mint, with a light aftertaste. It was an unexpected flavor, but the second mouthful tasted better than the first, and the third better than the second, so Haruhiro started to get the sense it might be really, really good.

"Setoran, you're good at cookin'!" Yume, who seemed to be going for a speed-eating award, said, rubbing her belly after she finished.

"Am I?" Setora asked, not sounding especially happy. "I do think that if I'm forced to eat something disgusting, I'd rather eat nothing at all. For something like this, you just prepare it in a way that won't cause food poisoning, then adjust the flavor in a way that will make it taste better."

"I don't think that's as easy as you're making it sound..." Merry muttered.

"Right?" Yume said in agreement. "Even if Yume does it thinkin', 'Be tasty, be tasty,' it ends up turnin' out kinda weird a lot of the time."

"I don't understand." Setora tilted her head. "The taste of things is decided. There are no uncertain elements in how the flavor will turn out if you mix them in certain proportions, and cook or boil them. Incidentally, when you say you think, 'Be tasty'...is that a wish? What meaning is there in doing that?"

"Um, well, if you're thinkin', 'Be tasty,' it's probably gonna turn out better than if you're thinkin', 'Be yucky.' Even if you do all the same stuff."

"If you truly do only the same things, no matter what you're thinking, the result will be the same. Rather than think meaningless things, you would do better to focus on the process."

"...Hmm. See, the thing about that, you may be right, but..."

"So, basically, Setora-san..." Kuzaku tried to help push the conversation forward. "You've got sense. Weren't you just born with a superior sense of taste?"

GRIMGAR OF FANTASY AND ASH

"I simply learned," she responded coolly. "Identifying the tastes one by one. The same with combinations of ingredients. There's little difference in what we were born with."

Whoops, it looks like the two of them are kind of missing each other's point, Haruhiro couldn't help but think. *I mean, Setora was born into a family of necromancers, the House of Shuro, and she's actually made a golem, and she's also a master nyaa tamer. Her cooking's good, too. Or rather, it's not just her cooking.*

"Setora, you're pretty good with a weapon, as well..." Haruhiro pointed out.

"Have to be able to defend myself," Setora explained as if it were nothing. "Swords, spears, bows, I can use most weapons. Nyaas are raised by onmitsu spies, so I've also learned some onmitsu techniques."

"You can do everything..." Kuzaku said, gaping, but Setora raised an eyebrow as if displeased.

"I've not learned so much that I can proudly say I'm able to do everything. However, I'm sure I'd not lose out to the foolish samurai warriors and onmitsu spies of the village. That's all."

"I feel like...that's pretty amazing by itself..." Shihoru's face was twitching.

"I guess you have a high capacity for learning," Haruhiro said. "Yeah. Somehow, that's the sense I get..."

For Haruhiro's part, he was just trying to vaguely sum things up, but Setora said, "No one has ever said that of me, and I don't think it, either," sounding upset for some reason. "Discovering unknown techniques would be one thing, but if there are people

28

who have done them before, you need only observe carefully, and the key points will come to you on their own. If they practice those key points, anyone can reach a certain level."

"No, but still?" Kuzaku daringly continued to ask questions. "There's gotta be things you're suited and unsuited to doing, right? There have to be things where, no matter how much you practice, you never improve."

"You need only practice until you become able to do them."

"You picked all this stuff up with hard work like that, Setora-san?"

"That goes without saying. You only get out what you put in. That is an ironclad rule."

"With the sword, too?"

"Naturally, there was a time when I did nothing but swing the sword, even cutting into my sleep time. If I didn't do that much, at least, I'd never get a feel for the hilt, would I?"

"...Is that how it works?"

"Rather than trying to learn the easy way, doing it the hard way tends to be simpler."

"Ohhh. Well, yeah. I can see that. Now that you say it, you may be right..." Kuzaku didn't seem to be able to say anything to that, and he was halfway to tears.

Most likely, Setora was right. She hadn't said anything too out there. In fact, it was common sense. It wasn't that you just needed to work hard; you needed to figure out the trick, and work hard in an efficient way. That was what Setora was telling him. Haruhiro couldn't argue with that.

But it's the kind of thing we ordinary people can't do, even if we wanted to. If we could do anything we set our minds to, anybody could be a superhero, right? But we're weak, frail, or lazy, and can't do things even if we want to. Sometimes, they'll feel like, "Ugh, I've had enough. I don't want to do anything." I could explain to Setora that's how people tend to be, but she'd just say, "Just do it." Yeah. She'd be right. If you don't do anything, nothing gets started, so the conclusion is you have to do it, right?

"Don't misunderstand." Setora hugged her knees and looked away. "I think what I am saying is correct. But just because it's correct doesn't mean people will accept it. I know that from experience. Even so, I won't bend from my opinion. If I lie about my own feelings, I'll cease to be myself..."

Haruhiro gulped. Yume, Shihoru, Merry, and Kuzaku were all surprised in their own ways, too.

What? What? What? What? Out of nowhere? Why? Setora, why are you crying...?

Haruhiro and Kuzaku looked at one another.

What's going on? I don't know. What do you think we should do? I don't know.

That sort of silent exchange happened between them in an instant.

We're so useless at times like this.

That was the shared conclusion the two of them came to.

"Umm, listen, Setoran..." Yume sat next to Setora, rubbing her back hard.

Yume, she's the one to handle things at a time like this.

As he watched, a little relieved, Haruhiro tried thinking about how Setora had been through a lot, too. Of course she had. After all, in the village, Setora had been a disgrace to the House of Shuro, treated as an outcast, living on the edge of the village with her nyaas. It wasn't as if she wouldn't have a few memories that might bring her to tears just thinking about them.

Unlike Haruhiro and the others, Setora had a homeland. However, even if the village was her homeland, it might not be a place she ought to return to. Enba the golem had been like a friend to her, but she had lost him. Of all the nyaas she had been raising, now only Kiichi was left.

It would be great if he could say to her, *It's okay, you have us, we're comrades, you're not alone,* but Haruhiro and Setora's relationship was a little complicated.

No, was Haruhiro only thinking it was complicated? Maybe it might not actually be? Which was it, really?

"You love that woman, I see."

That time, when Setora had said that to him, how had Haruhiro responded?

He remembered thinking he couldn't lie to her. If he recalled, he hadn't said it outright. Before he could finish telling her it was a one-sided affection, or something like that, Setora had covered Haruhiro's mouth with her hands. As if saying, *"I don't want to hear any more. Don't say anything."*

Haruhiro looked at Merry. Merry was still staring into the flames. She had no real expression.

Merry suddenly reached out towards the flames with her right hand.

Haruhiro was surprised and panicked. "M-Merry?"

She didn't act surprised, just slowly stopped her hand. Then, looking at her own fingers, she grabbed her right hand with her left. Then, after that, she turned to look at Haruhiro.

"What?"

"No, what was that, just now...?" Haruhiro was at a loss for how to respond.

What's gotten into you? You're acting kind of weird, Merry. You're concerned or worried about something, I'm sure. Talk to me. I'll listen. I mean, I want to hear it. Why can't I come out and say that?

"The dead don't come back."

He couldn't get Setora's words out of his head.

Jessie. That bizarre man had said it.

"This isn't normal. It's common sense that people can't come back to life, and that's a fact."

Right. That was a special event that happened under special circumstances. But Jessie had also said something else. That nothing had changed dramatically inside him when he'd come back to life. That there might be a little change, but nothing dramatic.

Most likely, Merry wasn't used to that little change yet. That was why she felt a little off, and might be confused. It was a transitional period, you could say.

He was about to say it was nothing, trying to dodge the subject, when Kiichi rushed in from the dark of night.

Setora pushed Yume away and stood up. Kiichi wrapped himself around Setora, meowing in a high-pitched voice.

"It looks like Kiichi found something," Setora said. "It would seem we had better get away from here."

"Kuzaku, put out the fire," Haruhiro ordered.

"'Kay!" Kuzaku stomped out their campfire.

Everyone picked up their gear. They were ready to go in no time at all.

"I hope we can sleep at least a little before dawn comes..." Shihoru said with a sigh, but from the wry grin on her face, it was clear she was half-joking.

Even Shihoru, who was less physically fit as a mage, wasn't so weak that this was going to get her down. They were a party of ordinary people, Setora aside, but for some reason they had led lives it would be hard to call ordinary as volunteer soldiers. Thanks to that, they'd trained up a decent amount.

Life is full of ups and downs, mountains and valleys. Uh, actually, it's just mountains lately, I guess. Really, there's been a lot that's happened. Still, we're alive, Manato, Moguzo.

That he could address his departed friends in his heart like this was just one more thing he could do because he was alive.

Grimgar
of
Fantasy and Ash

3 | Night Monster

SO, THE THING KIICHI FOUND...this is it, huh?

Haruhiro was standing in the shadow of a tree, holding his breath and making sure he had the right grip on his dwarven dagger.

Had this dagger really been made over a hundred years ago? It was hard to believe.

He'd often heard how wonderful the techniques of dwarven smiths were, and it didn't look like they fell short of their reputation. Aside from the intricate designs on the blade and hilt, it was an ordinary dagger, but when he held it, he could tell the difference.

The balance was good. It was clearly going to be easy to use. It also only took a little sharpening before a smooth texture appeared. The one he had called the flame dagger had a unique shape, but there seemed to be a hidden secret to it. It felt right when he swung it, and it cut really well.

Having good weapons in hand, that was reassuring. It was like having an invisible pillar standing up in the center of his body. If he got into trouble, he could lean on that pillar, which wouldn't be budged easily.

Something interrupted his concentration. There was the sound of something heavy being dragged, and of hard things scraping together.

Haruhiro's comrades had already withdrawn to the nearby ridge. He had come here to scout alone. That said, he didn't have the guts to get too close, and it wasn't necessary. He hadn't come all the way down from the ridge.

They were about ten meters below, moving through a valley.

The clouds drifted, and the moonlight shone down.

He saw what they were.

Humans, huh? That, or a race similar to humans. They were probably armed. He couldn't call their pace fast. It was slow as if they were completely exhausted at times, and strangely awkward at others. For some of them, one shoulder seemed unnaturally lowered, or the entire body tilted to one side, like a procession of defeated soldiers wounded in battle. This must be what they called a dead man's parade.

They were dead men. Not one was alive. They were moving corpses.

If he were to categorize them, the ones that still had flesh—rotting or not—were zombies, and the ones who had been reduced to just bones were skeletons. But whether they were skeletons or zombies, if you thought about it normally, their nerves and muscles couldn't be functioning properly, so they wouldn't be able to move.

They shouldn't be moving.

People said that the curse of No-Life King made it possible, but what exact mechanism was moving them? Or were they being manipulated like puppets?

Haruhiro decided he wanted to get a bit closer. No, that was wrong. He wanted to test something.

He took a deep, deep breath.

There were three basic techniques he needed to use.

First: eliminate his presence with Hide.

Second: move with Swing while his presence was eliminated.

Third: utilize all of his senses to detect the presences of others with Sense.

To describe it with an image, it was like this.

He'd sink beneath the ground without a sound. Once he dove in, it was less like being underground and more like being under the sea. He could move freely. Then, putting just his eyes and ears above the surface, he would look at, listen to, and feel all the things above the ground.

Stealth. He'd have been able to get into it. Before.

But this was no good.

He could get to a good place. He was almost there. If he could get past it, he'd be in. Despite that, something was holding Haruhiro back.

Naturally, Stealth wasn't that simple to do. But he'd been able to do it. For a time, he'd even been able to flip it on and off in an instant.

Haruhiro had the feeling of what it was like to be fully in Stealth firmly embedded in his mind. His field of vision quickly expanded, he saw things he couldn't see before, he heard things he couldn't hear, and he could even touch and feel things at a distance. He saw and heard so much, his consciousness leaving his body, that it gave him an illusion like he was looking down at himself and the area around him at an angle.

Not bad, he had thought. *Even a mediocre human like me can do this sort of thing if I try hard and stubbornly enough. The potential that people hold is amazing.*

But now...

I can't go there now. It may be one—no—a half-step away, but that difference is huge. The difference between being able to enter it and not is just too big of a difference. If I can enter Stealth properly, I can't even sneak up behind enemies that are searching for me with the intent to kill. It doesn't even feel like I might screw up. If the enemy is about to turn, I know it like the back of my hand.

Haruhiro ducked down.

Is this what they call a slump? he wondered.

When had it started? Had there been some trigger for it?

There had been. Possibly.

While being chased by the guorellas, they had fled into a jail-like building, despite the approaching guorellas still needing to be dealt with.

The leader. He had needed to take down the guorellas' leader.

In order to do that, he'd tried to go into Stealth, but likely because of his exhaustion, he hadn't been able to do it well.

Then *that* had happened to Merry.

A presence jerked him away from his memories. He thought his heart was going to stop.

Haruhiro inhaled as he leapt into the air, his dagger at the ready.

Merry was standing there, eyes wide, no more than three meters away from Haruhiro. She looked awfully surprised, but Haruhiro was, too. Or rather, Haruhiro was far more surprised.

"Wha..." he burst out.

No, no. They couldn't talk loudly here. The valley just beneath them was full of zombies and skeletons.

Haruhiro approached Merry, taking care not to make loud footsteps.

"Why are you here?" he whispered.

Merry hung her head in thought for a bit, and then almost-whispered back, "I was worried. You were acting a bit weird, Haru."

"Huh? Really? I don't think so."

"I could have been imagining it. Sorry."

"N-no need to apologize... Did you come here alone?"

"Yes."

"Okay." Haruhiro nodded vaguely.

Merry started to walk. She soon stopped. From there, she could look down into the valley.

"The dead..." she murmured.

"Yeah." Standing beside Merry, Haruhiro went to sheathe his dagger, then stopped, adjusting his grip on the weapon. Then he sheathed it after all. "I hear it's No-Life King's curse, though."

"Do you think that, Haru?"

"I can't say. They do call it a curse, though."

"I..." Merry bit her lip.

Her jaw was trembling. It had to hurt. Her lip, it was going to bleed. He wanted to say something. But for some reason, he couldn't. Merry was staring intently at the dead.

Suddenly, a thought occurred to Haruhiro. Maybe it wasn't him she was worried about, but she wanted to see the dead for herself. But, if so, for what reason?

"There must be something wrong with me," Merry whispered. "I'm making everyone worry. I know that."

"Yeah, we worry about you. Of course. We're comrades, after all. We have to care."

"It's probably just that it doesn't feel right. Even though I'm me."

"I... Nothing's going to change between us."

"I know that, too."

Merry still had her eyes on the dead. Without looking at Haruhiro, she smiled just a little.

"Shihoru and Yume, they both lend me a shoulder when I need one. And Kuzaku, he's not avoiding me. Of course, you aren't, either. I think Setora is a good person, too. Her gray nyaa is cute, after all. It's just...it feels like a lie. I'm a little afraid to go to sleep. This is going to sound cliché, but I don't know what I'd do if this was all a dream. If this is a dream, I want to make it clear to myself what is real and what is a dream. But I'm scared. I don't want to know."

"Merry..."

"I may be running away. I think I shouldn't run away. I... There's something wrong with me. I'm sure...I've changed. But I don't want to think so. If I'm messed up, I want you to tell me. I'm scared to hear it, but I'm just as scared you won't tell me."

"Listen, Merry..."

"I want you to stop me. I'm supposed to be here, but it's like I'm somewhere else. Where am I? I know. I'm here. And yet I don't know. It's not always, but there are times I just don't know. The wind is strong, and I feel like I'm going to be blown away. Where am I? Someone tell me. I—"

If he let her go on, Merry's voice was going to get louder and louder. In the end, she'd be shouting. That would be a little too much.

He had to do something. Could Haruhiro really say that was the only thing he was thinking? It was a sudden thing, and he couldn't explain it in detail, but it was like he was feeling this, this, and this, so he did this. He couldn't help but do it.

He hugged Merry.

For Haruhiro, in that moment, hugging Merry was the only option.

Well, he might be an idiot, but Merry wasn't. She acted reflexively to protect herself. Because of that, her arms were now in between the two of them.

Should I let go? Haruhiro wondered. *If anything, I have to let go. That's obvious, isn't it? What am I doing, hugging her like this? I'm not just an idiot; I'm an honest-to-goodness idiot.*

But Merry didn't move her arms. Didn't budge. Didn't try to push Haruhiro away.

Merry was tall for a woman, and Haruhiro wasn't big. But...

She sure is a girl, he thought.

Maybe it was the bone structure, or the muscle mass. Those things had to be different between men and women. Whatever the reason, even when he hugged her straight-on like this, Merry fit snugly into Haruhiro's arms.

The thought that he could protect her, could keep her rooted... honestly, he didn't think that one bit. Haruhiro didn't think he had the right, the abilities, or the capacity to do such a thing.

If he set aside the question of whether he was capable of it or not, though, he wanted to protect her, of course. That was what made him all the more scared, numbing his legs, so he couldn't take a step.

No, that wasn't it. It wasn't that he couldn't take a step; it was that he didn't want to.

"You're right here, Merry," he murmured. "Next to me. You don't need to think you don't know where you are, and I won't let you. Because I can sense you're right here, Merry."

He was scared, worrying he'd blurt out something strange. He couldn't remember the words a moment after they'd left his mouth in this state, so he couldn't even decide if they were weird or not.

Merry let out a sigh. Her body was hardly tense at all anymore. "I've always wanted you to do this."

Before asking, *Huh? What does that mean?* Haruhiro brought his lips up to a spot a little above Merry's left ear. Merry shuddered, and she let out a sigh.

His face was buried in Merry's hair. He could smell her scent.

Oh, crap. Am I acting like a deviant? Or maybe not? Having no experience to draw from, Haruhiro didn't know where this act fell on that scale. *I feel like I'm doing something pretty bold. I think any more would be too much.*

Would it be? Was this the limit? Having come this far, and trying this hard, was Haruhiro going to end up regretting this later?

I mean, we might never get into a situation like this again. Probably, we won't, right? Merry didn't seem to be put off by it. Probably. In that case, shouldn't I try to push on to the next thing? ... Next? What comes next?

Uhhh.

I dunno. Not about that. Could I take this back with me to think on? No? I can't? It has to be now? Only now? Well, yeah. Of course.

"Do you wanna..." he began.

What had Haruhiro been about to ask her? Was he going to ask her that? Really ask her? Merry? He wasn't so sure about that. There was no two ways about it. He couldn't ask. No. Absolutely not. Even Haruhiro knew that much.

"...head back?"

There was a momentary pause.

"Sure." Merry nodded, then suddenly smiled.

Somehow, it felt wrong to say, *I'm sorry,* but right now, Haruhiro desperately wanted to apologize. He wanted to pull off a kowtow that would put the legendary kowtow master to shame.

He wouldn't though, okay? There was no way he would. He couldn't do that, right?

Haruhiro backed away, releasing Merry from his arms. He wanted to bow apologetically, at least. No, he wasn't going to do it, though. But his body was honest. His face had turned downwards on its own.

"I'm sure everyone is waiting," she said.

If Merry hadn't said that for him, Haruhiro would never have been able to walk away from there.

Haruhiro and Merry returned to the ridge where their comrades were. Shihoru and Yume were sitting with their backs against a tree, leaning against each other and snoring softly. Kuzaku was half-asleep, too, but when he noticed Haruhiro and Merry he just said, "Oh..." and waved slightly.

What was that attitude for? What was up?

Kiichi may have been out looking around, because he was nowhere to be seen.

Setora was the only one standing.

"Oh, it's you two," she said briskly. "That was quick."

"...Oh?" Haruhiro asked nervously. "Really?"

Huh? What's that supposed to mean? Fast at what? Why?

He couldn't ask.

Haruhiro had an awfully sleepless night that night.

Grimgar
of
Fantasy and Ash

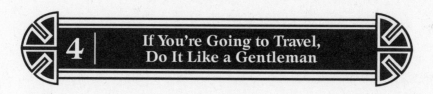

4 | If You're Going to Travel, Do It Like a Gentleman

SETTING ALL OF THAT ASIDE, Haruhiro and the party were heading more or less towards the east.

If they continued east, they knew they would hit the sea. If they followed the coast south from there, eventually they'd reach the free city of Vele. There were people who came and went between Vele and Alterna. If they joined up with a caravan, or took a job as bodyguards, they could return to Alterna.

It was a rough plan, but it was something. This was enemy land, far from the domain of the human race. There were no maps, so there was no way to plan things out precisely.

While procuring food and potable water, they headed east. They were on a mountain path, or rather a mountain where there were no paths to be found. It just wasn't possible to go due east, and north was out of the question, so they headed on a more or less southwards course.

But the mountains were crazy.

This area would most likely be considered part of the Kuaron Mountains. However, the mountains weren't that high. It was like an uninterrupted line of thousand-meter class mountains and several-hundred-meter class mountains.

That was the tricky part. The ups and down were intense. When the slopes were steep, it could be hard to climb or descend quickly, or outright impossible to do so at all. Even after zigzagging along for more than ten kilometers, they might only have moved a few kilometers in horizontal distance. That sort of thing was a regular occurrence.

Even so, the land was finally starting to level out. And when they first saw the shining surface of the water stretching from east to south, as far as the eye could see, Kuzaku let out a whoop and jumped into the air, shouting, "That's the sea, isn't it?!"

Haruhiro understood how he felt. He was happy, too. He wasn't about to start whooping, though.

Suddenly, he was fired up.

Still, haste would only make waste, so it was best not to pick up the pace. One of Haruhiro's all too few virtues was his ability to maintain control of himself at times like this. There was no idiot here to tell him, *You're such a buzzkill! That's what makes you no fun, you reject!* So he'd hold in that desire, repress it, and move forward slowly but surely.

"Hey, hey!" Just ten meters up ahead, Yume was up on top of a small, rounded hill, waving both her arms. "Do you think we can stop to eat here? The wind's blowin' reeeal hard, and it feels purrrrfect!"

Dusk was approaching. Even if they hadn't been rushing, Yume was pretty energetic considering they had been walking nonstop for about half a day.

"I'd think the food would be the same no matter where we ate it..." Setora seemed exasperated, but she briskly walked over and began preparing for meal time just in front of the hill. "You there, loyal dog. Start a fire."

"'Kay." Kuzaku responded immediately, but once he started setting up the fire, he paused.

"...Wait, loyal dog?" He tilted his head to the side. "At the very least, I don't recall being your dog, Setora-san. Not me. Do something about the way you address me, 'kay?"

"I cannot, 'kay?"

"Don't imitate me..."

"Then shut up, and do as you're told. I am busy. Don't interrupt me, loyal dog."

"Ugh, it makes me want to just start barking..."

If you have to bark, then bark, my friend, Haruhiro called out to his loyal dog in his heart, then turned a subtle glance towards Merry.

Was something up, or was it a coincidence? Merry was looking Haruhiro's way as well. Because of that, their eyes met.

Now, what to do?

If he were a traveling gentleman, he ought to say, *Oh, why, hello! What a coincidence this is! Ha ha ha!* However, Haruhiro was not a gentleman traveler. Or rather, what *was* a gentleman traveler?

Haruhiro and Merry were staring into one another's eyes. However, ultimately, that was the only thing that was happening, and there was no special meaning behind it. If Merry turned her eyes away like nothing had happened, Haruhiro would have thought nothing of it. It was likely the same for Merry.

Probably, at least? Haruhiro wasn't Merry, so he couldn't say for certain. That was why, no matter what, he didn't want her to think, *Oh, am I being avoided, maybe?* There was no way he would avoid her, now was there? Jeez.

Merry might have been thinking the same way, and it was making it hard to be the first to look away. In case she was, Haruhiro would work up the courage to be first. No, but he didn't want to create a misunderstanding.

Shihoru was slowly working her way up the hill. Haruhiro could see her out of the corner of his eye.

Hold on, hold on! Hey! Say something here! Shihoru! Come on. Like, "What are you doing?" or "What's up?" or something. If you'd just say anything, give me a chance to respond, I could say, "Huh, what?" and get out of this stalemate.

Why were they being left alone? Could it be they were being shunned? Everyone was secretly conspiring against them? Haruhiro and Merry were being pushed out? Left out? No way. That couldn't be it, right? Nuh-uh. Not a chance.

"Noooo?" Yume let out a sound.

Nice one, Yume. I can play this off as catching my attention, Haruhiro thought, and actually did that.

Yume cocked her head to the side, looking down at her feet. "Hurrrm? Just now, somethin'..."

"Eek!" Shihoru, who was still mid-climb, let out a little scream.

Kuzaku jumped back. "Shihoru-san?! What's wrooooooong?!"

"Wha..." Setora said, looking up at the hill.

Haruhiro looked, too. Was it...a hill? It might not have been. At the very least, it was no ordinary hill. The truly hill-like hill, the one everyone expects when they hear the word "hill," doesn't move, right?

"Meow, meow, meooow..." Yume was stumbling around on top of the hill. Or rather, was she trying to catch her balance so as not to fall down?

The grass-covered hill, which was maybe ten to fifteen meters across, and around ten meters high, was stirring.

"Eeeek..." Shihoru was clinging on to the bumpy slope, letting out a distressed wail. She was halfway up, so that put her at about five meters off the ground.

"Hey, jump down, mage!" Setora shouted.

At Setora's feet, Kiichi with his gray fur standing on end was hissing and baring his fangs.

"I-It's one thing to say that, but..." Shihoru burst out.

"Hurry it up! That hill is alive! Hunter, you get down while you still can, too!"

"Hungh!" Yume, always quick to act, immediately began racing down the hill.

Shihoru was looking down, hesitant.

"What do you mean, the hill's alive?" Haruhiro shook his head to clear it. "No, now's not the time. Shihoru, Setora's right! Kuzaku, catch Shihoru!"

"Woof!" Kuzaku called.

"And now he's barking..."

"It just happened, okay?! Shihoru-san! Come on, it's going to be all right! I'll catch you!"

Kuzaku got right beneath Shihoru and spread his arms wide.

The hill was alive. What did that mean? It wasn't just stirring; it was changing its form, too. From the start, even if it was somewhat bumpy, it had been a rounded hill on the whole. But not now. Now it bulged out in some places, and in others, it pulled back in. In response to that, like a little landslide, the dirt and grass that was rooted in those spots came tumbling down loudly.

"Shihoru!" Merry pressed her.

Immediately afterwards, maybe finally having made up her mind, Shihoru took off from the slope. The place she had been standing a moment before caved in, so it was a close call.

Kuzaku caught Shihoru.

"Get back!" Haruhiro backed away himself as he gave the order. He hadn't meant to pull back, but he did it despite himself.

The hill was alive. Was this what that meant? The hill was in the process of standing up.

Naturally, hills didn't stand up. If it was a normal hill—no—even an abnormal hill, it really shouldn't have been standing up. That meant it wasn't a hill to begin with. It was a creature.

There it had been, bent over, likely for a very, very long time.

Exposed to wind and rain, and covered in dirt and dust, eventually plants had taken root. In the end, it had been reduced to a hill-like state.

"It's big," Merry mumbled.

Yeah. I know, right?

It first knelt, then half rose, and was attempting to stand upright, but its back was hunched like an old person's, and it couldn't get its torso up that well. There were still copious amounts of dirt and grass clinging to it. In spots, it even looked to have become one with the grass and dirt. Had the grass put down roots into its skin, maybe?

But it was human. Well, humanoid. Its body was shaped like Haruhiro's or anyone else in the party's. There was a massive size difference, though. Because looking at it, even with its back hunched, it had to be over fifteen meters, maybe even twenty meters tall, right?

"I've heard of these," Setora said. "It's a forest giant."

At some point, Setora had brought Kiichi and was standing at Haruhiro's side. When Haruhiro looked at the side of her face, Setora sidestepped away, for some reason.

"They are a type of giant race, and I have heard that they can live for hundreds of years, sleeping like beasts in hibernation... I never thought they actually existed, though."

"Ah, wah, wah, wah, wah!" Kuzaku was running this way, still carrying Shihoru.

Haruhiro's eyes went wide. "Ah! Hold on, Ku—"

The forest giant reached out its arm, seeming to fall as it did.

Kuzaku. It was aiming for Kuzaku.

Huh? What, what, what? If it caught him, what would it do? Eat him or something? Was it feeling a little peckish after its long sleep?

"Wahhhhhhhhhhhhh!" Kuzaku wailed as he pumped his legs for all they were worth.

Shihoru clung to Kuzaku, shrieking, "Eeeeeeeeeeeeeeeek!"

Haruhiro wanted to save them. But his opponent was too large. He couldn't stop a thing like that, no matter what he tried. Even so, he'd have to do something. That was because Kuzaku and Shihoru were his precious comrades, and Haruhiro was the leader.

But if he were to be fully honest, Haruhiro's thinking was completely frozen, up to the point where he was thinking only, *Isn't this kind of impossible?* At this point, Haruhiro was no more than a bystander.

"Delm, hel, en, balk, zel, arve!"

Chanting. It was a spell.

Not Shihoru. It was Merry.

Merry chanted a spell and activated magic. It was the Blast Spell of Arve Magic. An explosion rose from the face of the forest giant. The forest giant stumbled. It looked like it might fall...no, it was actually falling. Its massive body tilted forward, and it kept going until it slammed into the ground.

Kuzaku and Shihoru were okay. It had been a pretty risky situation, but they'd somehow managed not to get snatched by the forest giant.

Haruhiro waved his arms. "Everyone, run!"

Setora and Kiichi took off. Yume looked like she was planning to take off in another direction temporarily, then catch up with the group later. Kuzaku was coming along with Shihoru in his arms.

"Merry?!" Haruhiro shouted.

When he looked over, Merry had a hand pressed to her forehead, her eyes shut, and was gritting her teeth. She looked to be in pain.

When he rushed over and put a hand on her shoulder, Merry replied, "Yeah. I'm fine," but she didn't look it one bit.

If it weren't a situation like this, he'd want her to lie down and have a rest, or at least sit down and drink some water. Unfortunately, that wasn't an option now. The forest giant wasn't unharmed, but it was trying to get up.

Haruhiro took Merry by the hand. Her hand was cold. When he gripped it tight, she gripped back.

The two took off running in silence.

Grimgar of Fantasy and Ash

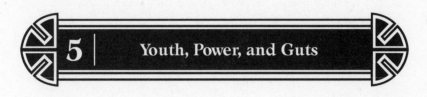

5 | Youth, Power, and Guts

*W*E WENT EASTWARD, Haruhiro narrated silently. *Then,
along the way, southeastward.*

*It wasn't all fun times. In fact, it was very rarely fun times, but
it wasn't all bad times, either. Like, in a raging storm, we'd generally
come across a cave that we could take shelter in. Then the weather
would clear up, and it would feel refreshing, like the whole thing
had been a lie.*

*The food Setora makes can be really tasty, too. Kiichi gets temperamental, but he'll nuzzle up to us, purr when petted, and be cute. There
is a surprising amount of happiness that could be found lying about
here and there. I just had a pretty hard time spotting it was there.*

*This journey has taught me things. It may not have been a
bad trip.*

Haruhiro went on with his internal monologue, getting up to
the point of, *This is how our journey ended.*

"So this is the sea, huh?" Setora said quietly.

Kiichi stuck close to her feet, his raised tail swaying back and forth gently.

"It sure is the sea..." Yume narrowed her eyes and grinned.

Shihoru squatted down and let out a sigh. "Phew..."

"Haruhiro." Kuzaku was facing this way. A serious look on his face.

"What is it?"

"You mind if I shout?"

"Huh? You want to shout? Well, I don't see a problem..."

"Right, I'm gonna shout, then."

Kuzaku cupped his hands in front of his mouth like a trumpet, leaned back, took a deep breath, and then...

"It's the seaaaaaaaaaaaaaaaaaaaaaaaaaaaaaaaaaaaaaaaaaaaa...!"

"He sounds like an idiot," Merry murmured.

Haruhiro agreed entirely, but he kind of understood how Kuzaku felt.

Haruhiro and the party were looking out over the sea from the final mountain peak. They had to be about three hundred meters above sea level. Once they descended this mountain, they'd be at the shore. From there, the boundless blue sea stretched out as far as the eye could see.

Haruhiro had had enough of mountains. He'd climbed up and down enough of them for one lifetime. Finally, at long last, this was the final one.

The previous day, with this last peak before their eyes, they deliberately chos to camp out without ascending it fully. They'd been so excited that they got up while it was still dark out to watch the sunrise from the summit.

Ultimately, it took more time to ascend the summit than anticipated, so they weren't able to see the moment the sun rose from beyond the horizon. But despite missing the first light, it was still a marvelous sight. If Haruhiro were inclined to poetry, he'd probably have composed a verse or two.

"...Yeah, I've got nothing," he commented.

"For what?" Merry asked.

"Oh, no, nothing..."

Even as the shadows cast by the dim sky fell upon her, Merry shone in the dawn light. If he were a poet, he could sing her praises with beautiful words.

He murmured, "So pretty your mind goes blank."

"I know, right?" Merry looked at the sea, letting out a little sigh.

Haruhiro hadn't meant the sea, though. Nor had he meant the sun, which shone like a billion jewels were scattered over its surface. He'd been referring to Merry.

"By the way, Haru." Setora was glaring.

"...Yes?"

"When I look at you, I occasionally—quite often, in fact— find myself frustrated to the point that I want to kill something."

"That's not very nice..."

"It's not. Do be careful that I don't kill you."

"Um... I'd love to be careful and all, but what exactly do you want me to..."

For some reason, Kuzaku squatted down beside Shihoru, and barked like a dog. "Woof!"

Shihoru patted Kuzaku on the back, and on his head, too. Was his dogification progressing faster and faster?

This is apparently all my fault somehow. That much Haruhiro could guess. *But, hey, what can I do? I'd love to do something about this indecisive personality of mine, you know? If I could change, I would, and I do try to take steps forward when I can, but it's probably not enough. More, huh? I need to do more. On the other hand, if I do take a decisive step, there's the problem that I don't know what will happen. Like, what influence it will have on everyone around me. I'm still the leader, you know? I can't not think about that. There's that to consider, so it's not easy. It's hard. Life is too hard...*

"By the way, y'know?" Yume pointed in the direction of the sea. "Over there, there's somethin' like a ship. It's tilted, isn't it? Or is Yume just imaginin' that?"

No, that definitely wasn't her imagination. How far from the beach was it? Not close, but not that far. That sailboat wasn't sailing, so it might be fair to say it was stopped, but something was strange about it. Like Yume had said, it was clearly tilted.

"Has it run aground?" Haruhiro wondered aloud.

Whatever the case, they couldn't make a call on it from here. Haruhiro and the party descended the mountain towards the sea. Thinking this was the last mountain, it made him want to hum a little tune like he was on a picnic, but if they let their guards down, something would trip them up. That was what it meant to travel.

They descended the mountain in what felt like two hours, then walked for about thirty minutes and reached a grassy field overlooking a rocky beach.

The ship in question was dead ahead. Its sails were white, and the body was not aged. It didn't look to have been abandoned to rot there a long time ago, so it might have run aground recently. While this was an amateur analysis, that was the impression he got.

Incredibly, on the rock beach, there were people. No, he didn't know that they were human, but there were multiple humanoid creatures. More than ten of them, sitting, standing, and roaming around.

"Maybe they're the crew of that ship," he murmured.

Haruhiro and the party were in a straight line, lying down on the ground. The people over there most likely couldn't see them.

"Meow..." Yume squinted. Being a hunter, she had the best vision of any of them. "There're six men...maybe? Human men, that is. Oh, there's some non-humans, too? One might be an orc. Probably, at least. There're kobolds, too. Oh, and a gobbie? What's that one with the bandage wrapped around his face? Hard to tell. There's one girl, too... Hrmm. Is that a girl?"

If it were just humans, that would be one thing, but there were orcs, kobolds, and goblins, too. On top of that, there was one human woman mixed in with the bunch. Just what kind of group was this?

"I have heard that humans and orcs co-exist in Vele..." Setora sounded uncharacteristically uncertain.

There were too many uncertain elements. Was it better not to get involved? It was a curious sight, but curiosity had been known to kill, and a certain idiot who had once been with the party had brought a lot of trouble down on them with his.

Yeah, thought Haruhiro. *Let's not investigate it. We'll leave quietly, and pretend we didn't see anything.*

He said, "Creep to the rear, then head south..."

Maybe *creep to the rear* instead of *creep forward* was a weird way to word it. Haruhiro was about to correct himself when Yume made a strange noise.

"Huhwah!"

"Wh-what's wrong, Yume?"

"She's wavin'."

"Huh? Who is?"

"The girl... But that girl, she's got a mustache. Do girls grow mustaches? Yume's never grown a mustache."

"Well, maybe it depends on the per—Wait, huh? She's waving?"

Looking down, there most certainly was a person who looked like a girl waving in their direction. But was this one of those cases where he'd think, *Who, me?* and then it would turn out to be someone else? Like, was there was another of that girl's comrades behind Haruhiro and the party, maybe?

That would be dangerous, too. Yeah. Definitely dangerous. Haruhiro turned to check. Nope. No one there.

"Heyyyy!" the girl finally started shouting.

She was looking at them, wasn't she?

He'd have given it a better than eighty percent chance she was.

Ninety percent, maybe? It could be ninety-nine. Perhaps even one hundred.

"Heyyyy! You theeeere! Come ouuuut! If you're enemies, we'll kill youuuu!"

"D-do we fight?" Kuzaku went to draw his large katana.

"Wait," Haruhiro stopped him. If it was going to come to a fight, they should run instead. They were more than fifty meters from the group.

He was about to give the order to retreat when the mysterious bandaged man handed the girl a cylindrical object of some sort. What was that? The girl pointed that object towards them.

"Ka-boom!"

When the girl said that, there was a *ka-boom*, or a *bang*, and a *whoosh*, and Haruhiro pushed himself up with his arms. Had there been an impact just now? Something had flown this way, and hit the ground with incredible force. There was smoke rising from the end of the object the girl was holding.

"No way! Is that a firearm?" Shihoru took the words out of Haruhiro's mouth.

"Heyyyy! Come ouuuut! The next one's going to hiiiit! It'll hurt, tooooo! I'm one spicy sniper! Yes, indeedy! But not really, though!" The girl was babbling on and only half making sense.

"Was that...magic?" Even Setora was shocked. Kiichi was keeping low to the ground, and had begun a crawling retreat.

"No," Haruhiro said. "It's not magic. It's a weapon."

Haruhiro bit his lip and licked it. A firearm. Why a firearm? No, were firearms even a thing? He'd never seen one—right? In that case, why did Haruhiro, and Shihoru for that matter, know they existed, and what they were called? Was it their memories, knowledge from before they came to Grimgar?

Whatever the case, it was a weapon that propelled a bullet with gunpowder. A firearm. Also called a gun. Like the girl said, if a bullet struck them, they wouldn't get off lightly. Merry was here, so she could heal any wounds if they weren't fatal, but it was fully possible for a bullet to cause instant death if it hit them in the wrong spot.

"Don't shoot!" Haruhiro shouted and raised one hand. He rose to one knee. His comrades were still shaken, it seemed. He was sorry to be acting on his own initiative, but there was no choice. This was a crisis situation.

"If you come out, I won't shoooot!" The girl still had her gun at the ready. "But you aaaaall have to come out! Yes, indeed! I'm not blonde, after all! Oops, sorry! I meant bliiiiind!"

"What guarantee do we have you won't shoot?!" Haruhiro shouted.

"Uh, I promise not toooo! Pinky sweaaaar!"

"We can't pinky swear! Not this far away!"

"I guess noooot! But you'll just have to trust me, I gueeeess!"

"You say to trust you, but we don't even know who you are!"

"I don't know you eitheeeer! That makes us even, riiiight?! Yes, indeed!"

Her way of speaking included, she was a very strange woman, but she didn't seem to be an idiot. Would it be okay to tell her they were volunteer soldiers? This was enemy territory, after all, so it was a hard call.

"Haruhiro-kun!" Shihoru called his name.

When he looked over, Shihoru nodded.

Yeah, thought Haruhiro. She was right. There was no way to be certain about it, but these people probably didn't belong to an organization opposed to humanity. If they did, they would have attacked the party without hesitation the moment they spotted them.

"Everyone stand." Following Haruhiro's order, his comrades stood, one after another.

The girl threw the gun to the bandaged mystery man, and pointed a finger in their direction. "All riiiight! Now, one of you, get over here and face meeee! I don't care who, just bring it oooon! Yes, indeed!"

It would seem she was an even weirder woman than anticipated.

Haruhiro descended to the rock beach, facing off against the group.

The members of the group did indeed appear to be sailors. Well, not that he was an expert on sailors, but they seemed dressed for labor aboard a ship, and not just the humans but the orcs and goblins were tanned, too. They were exactly what you'd expect men of the sea to look like.

The girl was wearing a hat that rolled up on both sides and men's clothes, and she sported a mustache. No, was it a fake mustache? More than likely, yes. Even for Haruhiro, a man, if he left his mustache to grow, it probably wouldn't be as bushy as that.

Was she messing around?

It didn't feel like it, though.

The girl puffed up her chest, crossed her arms, and looked at Haruhiro and the party. Her gaze was sharp. Overwhelming even. Though she was petite, she had an intensity that didn't let them sense that.

"I am K&K's K! M! W! Momohina! Name yourselves!"

"...K&K?" Merry furrowed her brow.

Momohina's opened her eyes wide. "Name yourselves!" she repeated.

"Hey!" the men began shouting. "She said name yourself, idiot!"

"We'll kill the men and screw the women if you don't!"

"I wanna screw them anyway!"

"Now you're just letting your desires show, jerkface!"

This was awful. The girls in the group were intimidated. Kuzaku snapped and tried to move forward.

"Tie uuuup!" Momohina shouted, and the men closed their mouths.

Haruhiro was befuddled. Tie up...?

Momohina cleared her throat. "...Oops. The correct answer was 'shut up'! These things haaaappen. That's all from the scene. Indeed!"

Her face was red. She seemed embarrassed.

"Mm-hm..." Yume nodded in agreement.

Oh, you're going to sympathize with her there? Yeah, you would, I guess.

Yume and Momohina. These two had some strange similarities. But Yume wouldn't wear a fake mustache. She wouldn't fire off a gun, either. And she wouldn't issue a challenge out of nowhere.

"Um, when you say to face you, what do you mean?" Haruhiro asked, just to be sure.

Momohina, with her cheeks still flushed, grinned and gave a thumbs-up. "We're gonna throw down, mano-a-mano, obviously! You bet we are. Full speed ahead!"

"Full speed ahead!" The men echoed back with hoarse voices.

Mano-a-mano. That meant one-on-one. Bare-handed, then?

"You're on!" When Kuzaku spun his arm in a circle, moving forward, Momohina's mustache twisted and almost fell off.

"Duwhuh?!"

Momohina immediately pressed her fake mustache back on her face, but Kuzaku had lost his enthusiasm. Knowing Kuzaku, he'd remembered his opponent was a woman, and was wondering whether mano-a-manoing—no, that wasn't a word that existed—whether going mano-a-mano with a woman was okay.

Haruhiro wasn't keen on having a fistfight with a woman himself, but he wasn't sure about leaving it to the women in the group, either.

"Okay, I'll do it," he said.

"Heh heh," Momohina cackled. "Bring it on! This'll be a cakewalk. Yes, indeed!"

Momohina cast aside her coat. The men let out a cheer, and Haruhiro hurriedly turned to the side. Momohina had been wearing a knee-length coat, but, naturally, he had expected her to be wearing a shirt underneath. She wasn't. It was bare skin. She wasn't naked, but she only had a band tied around her breasts in place of underwear, so it was hard to look at her directly.

"What's wroooong? Heyyyy! Come at meeee!"

"Can you put the coat back on?" he asked.

"No way!"

"Why...?"

"It's too heavy to move iiiin! Do you understaaaand?! This feeeeling?!"

"I don't, really, but can you try to understand how I feel, too?"

"I don't care about that, so let's do this! Hoorah! If you won't come to me, maybe I should go on the attaaaack? Here I coooome!"

Momohina closed in. In an instant, Haruhiro went into work mode like a switch had been flipped, jumping back diagonally with all his strength.

Oh, crap. She's fast. What?

"Hee. Let me guess, you're no amateur, riiiight?"

That stance. Her left foot and hand were forward, her hips lowered, and her hand open slightly. There was no unused strength anywhere in her body. From a state that looked almost relaxed, she rapidly accelerated. She was the one who was no amateur.

"Entertain me!" she shouted. "Yes, indeed!"

Unlike with a punch or a slap, her arms, her wrists, and even her fingers flexed and assaulted him. Though this couldn't be the case, it felt like they'd cut him if they hit him. Haruhiro relied on his reflexes to avoid Momohina's attacks. If he tried to plan out what to do in his head in response to each move, he stood no chance of keeping up.

"Schwing, schwing, schwing, schwing, schwing, schwing, schwing, schwing, schwiiiiing!" she shouted.

What a fierce assault. Fast and flowing. It never let up.

Haruhiro quickly lost the ability to avoid it, and when he blocked with his arm, his arm wasn't so much knocked away as pushed aside, and he lost his balance. He was cornered in no time. He had no other moves left. Reluctantly, Haruhiro went on the counterattack.

Punching and kicking wasn't his specialty. He decided to take a combo attack from Momohina, withstand it, and try to grab her arm. A thief's fighting techniques included a skill called Arrest.

Now.

The moment he thought that, he was flipped over. His arm was grabbed instead, and he was thrown.

"So cloooose!"

Momohina was going for a shot at Haruhiro's face. Not with a fist, though. What did she plan to do with that unclenched hand? He didn't know, but he was sure that one attack would work.

He didn't do it intentionally. The limiter in his brain must have come undone by itself.

Assault.

Haruhiro jumped away from Momohina, then immediately sprang at her. He didn't think how to use his hands or feet, didn't think about feinting to get his real attacks in, none of that. He didn't look at his opponent's movements, or attempt to sense them. He cut off all his responses to just attack.

Attack.

His heart pounded, his blood vessels expanded to many times their normal size, and the blood coursed through his body at an unbelievable speed. It didn't matter that his opponent was female, or that she was human at all, to Haruhiro in his current state. Meat collided with and crushed meat. They could both be reduced to bloody pulp for all he cared. In fact, he wanted that. When attacking with Assault, Haruhiro was himself, but at the same time not himself.

Even so, it wasn't enough.

Momohina slipped past his right hand, his left hand, his right foot, and his left foot, turning them aside. She was toying with him. Like he was a child.

This is no good.

Momohina was a weird woman, but not an idiot. She must have known from the beginning that she would never lose a hand-to-hand fight. She had lured Haruhiro into a battle she was sure to win. The contest was already decided.

"Is that! The best! You! Can do?!" she shouted.

Having parried the attack Haruhiro had poured every last bit of strength into, she confidently went on the attack. Assault cast aside all reason, completely abandoning defense in order to focus on the attack. If she got him now, he had nothing to give back.

"Delm!" Momohina slammed her palm into Haruhiro's left flank. Though a direct hit was to his flank, it echoed all the way to the top of his head.

Even as he reeled, Haruhiro fiercely tried to grab her. Momohiro shouted "Hel!" and "En!" striking his left and right shoulders, then his solar plexus with "Balk!" The punishing blows were like stakes being driven into him. At this point, Haruhiro was already losing consciousness. The only thing keeping him on his feet was stubbornness, or guts, or coincidence.

"Zel!" Momohina stepped in, kicking Haruhiro's left knee.

He fell backwards. He couldn't keep his footing any longer.

"Arve!"

If Momohina had landed a clean hit on his chin with the palm she brought down, who knows what might have happened to Haruhiro. He might well have died.

Momohina deliberately chose not to hit him.

That wasn't all. Momohina used the right arm she'd made miss to hug the falling Haruhiro, and to spin him around. At the same time, *boom,* there was an explosion somewhere else.

Screams and cheers went up, and Momohina sat Haruhiro on the ground.

It must have come off at some point during the fight. Her fake mustache was gone.

Momohina's face was very much that of a young girl. Her real age was unknown, but she looked even younger than Haruhiro and his party. Wait, what had that explosion been just now? Could it have been Blast?

Delm, hel, en, balk, zel, arve... Come to think of it, she'd chanted a spell, hadn't she? Huh? Then what? Was she a mage?

"I am Momohina! The K&K Pirate Company's KMW! I'm a kung-fu master, a mage, and a woman! Woo!" she shouted.

The men threw their hands up and cheered with gruff voices. "Ooooooooooooh!"

K = Kung-fu Master. M = Mage. W = Woman.

Oh, so *that* was it. Well, it wasn't like there was any other KMW, so it was pretty much a straight description of her.

"How's that?!" Momohina looked down at Haruhiro arrogantly. She looked so...smug. "Flawless! Victory! Oh yeah! You admit defeat?"

"I admit defeat."

"Goooood! Now then, from here on, you people are my underlings! Under, under, underlings! Okay!"

"Huh? W-we are...?"

"You bet you are! By fighting mano-a-mano, we formed a bond of bloooood!"

"You say that like fighting makes friends. No, I guess that's not quite it..."

"It's fine, it's fine! Don't sweat the small stuff! Youth! Power! Guts! It's YPG! This is pirate law, okay?! Yes, indeed!"

"Pirates..."

Come to think of it, she'd been saying something about the K&K Pirate Company. The men were sailors, and Momohina was apparently their captain. Their ship was run aground over there.

Okay, then. This was a group of pirates. That was their pirate ship, and Momohina was the captain. Hence the mustache? No, she didn't really need one, did she?

"...Wait, we're underlings? To a pirate? Huh? Seriously?"

Grimgar
of
Fantasy and Ash

6 | Calcium

I N LIFE, you never know what will happen. No one knows what the future holds. In fact, that may be what life is all about.

"Okaaay! Next! To-wah!"

When Momohina struck a mysterious pose, Yume, Shihoru, Merry, and Setora—who were lined up in front of her—all shouted, "To-wah!" and struck the same pose.

"Next! Se-hah! Sah! Zan, zan! Yarya!"

When Momohina did a spinning kick, knifehand strike, two jabs, and a reverse spinning kick, Yume and the others mimicked her.

"Se-hah! Sah! Zan, zan! Yarya!"

Yume, Merry, and Setora were starting to get good, but Shihoru wasn't making any progress. It was hard to blame her. Shihoru was a mage, after all. Well, so was Momohina, but she was a special case, so it was probably fair to count her as an exception.

"Next! Chorya! Nata! Fumi! Shu, sha, briin!"

"Chorya, nata, fumi, shu, sha, briiin."

"You're lacking energy! Come on, make it snappy! Do-wah! Se-rah!"

"Do-wah! Se-rah!"

"Niiiice! Keep it uuuup!"

Kung-fu lessons on the beach continued. How had this happened? Haruhiro didn't really know. Regardless, Yume and the girls were learning kung-fu from Momohina, while Haruhiro and Kuzaku were doing manual labor with the other men.

Though they called it labor, all they were really doing was helping the sailors—which was to say, pirates—with things like combing the beach for things that had washed up, collecting firewood, and attempting to build shelters and rafts. There was no urgency to any of it, either.

There were a number of barrels from the beached pirate ship hauled ashore, and in them were salted fish, meat, and pickled vegetables, so food was no issue for the time being. For water, they could draw it from the nearby river and boil it to make it potable. If they really wanted to, they could even drink it straight from the river and, well, it probably wouldn't kill them.

The pirates were bored. If there was booze, they'd have drunk and partied, but it seemed they had already drank the last of it. With their hands idle, they were finding things to do for lack of any alternative. Maybe even killing time was too much hassle for them, because there was no shortage of pirates lying on top of the rocks and snoring.

However, Haruhiro and his group were the new guys, bottom of the hierarchy. If they rested, they'd be yelled at. "Hey, get to work!" It was boring to do nothing anyway, so they lent a hand to the pirates who were moving around.

While they were doing so, the sun went down. Once it was dark out, they lit a bonfire and posted guards, or didn't. Kiichi, who had been off somewhere doing whatever he pleased, returned. Eventually, the night ended and day broke. Yet another new day, indistinct from any other, had begun.

The pirate life was a little different from what Haruhiro had imagined.

No, not that he had ever imagined it. He'd never had ties with any pirates. Never thought he'd be involved with them, either. But here he was, a member of a pirate crew. But was this what a pirate crew did? Like, were they even doing anything? Maybe not.

Yume and the others spent all day practicing kung-fu. Though a more persuasive theory was that they were just going along with Momohina, who was playing teacher because she had too much time on her hands. Haruhiro and the others were her underlings, so if it was a request from the KMW of the K&K Pirate Company, or whatever she wanted to call herself, they had no right to refuse.

They had ended up in this position because of Haruhiro's losing a mano-a-mano fight, so he was reflecting deeply on what he did wrong. But, at this point, their life on the rocky beach was so relentlessly peaceful that reflecting on it was starting to feel downright stupid.

On the fifth day, a ship came.

The truth was, Momohina and her crew hadn't been hanging out on that rocky beach for no purpose. They'd been waiting for one of their comrades' ships.

The ship dropped anchor off shore, and sent out a dinghy. There were three pirates aboard it. Two were human, but one was, incredibly, a fishman.

"Momohina-saaan! It's me, me! Ginzy. Ginzy is here for you! Momohina-saaan, can you hear meee?! Ginzy is here to collect you, you know?!"

The orc, goblin, and kobold pirates all spoke the human language, even if highly accented at times, so maybe it shouldn't have been a surprise. However, it was. The proper term for his race might not be a fishman, but that pirate was pretty darn fish-like. He wore clothing with a design similar to Momohina's coat, along with a hat, but it was impressive how fish-like he was.

"Ohhh. Ginzy, huh...?" Momohina looked blatantly disappointed, even slightly upset. Considering that their fellow pirate, who they had waited all this time for, had finally shown up, she wasn't terribly excited.

"Give it up, KMW," the bandaged pirate said to Momohina. His name was Jimmy, and his position was apparently something like Momohina's assistant. "If we set her captain aside, the *Mantis-go* is a fine ship. With this, we can at least return to the Emerald Archipelago."

"Well, yeeeeah. You're right, buuuut..."

"Haven't you known Ginzy longer than me, KMW?"

"Listen, that means I've been made to listen to a whoo00le loooot more pointless drivel from him, okaaaay?"

"Oh, when you put it that way, that's pretty unbearable..."

"He always gets carried away, babbling on and ooooon. He wouldn't be a bad kid if he weren't so annoying, though. That Ginzy."

They were saying a lot of mean things about him, but when Ginzy the fishman disembarked from the dinghy onto the rocky beach, he seemed highly unlikable.

"Whew, sorry I'm later than planned. I'm terribly sorry, but, huh? What's this? Why am I not feeling very welcomed? Huh, huh, huh? That's weird. You think it's weird, too, right? I mean, I came here to get you, didn't I? Even if you ran into a storm, it took some real carelessness to run aground, and here I am, going out of my way to come collect you all. I won't demand you cry 'banzai' three times or anything, but a 'thank you' would seem appropriate, wouldn't you agree? No, no, I'm not going to turn back without you or anything, okay? Why I'd *never* do such a thing. It's not like I *couldn't*, though, you know? But I won't. I really won't. I mean it."

"What's with this guy?" When those words slipped out of Kuzaku's mouth, Ginzy's fish eyes glared in his direction.

"Huh?! That should be my line, you know?! I've never seen or eaten your face before, okay?! It'd be scary if I *had* eaten it, you say? That's just a sahuagin joke! Okay, that's the part where you laugh! I don't understand why your sides aren't splitting!"

"W-we're new." It looked like it was going to develop into something troublesome, so Haruhiro forced Kuzaku's head down, saying, "Go on, apologize." He then explained, "I lost to Momohina...the KMW...in a mano-a-mano showdown, so we're her underlings now...or something."

"Fishishishishishhhh?! You? Had a showdown with Momohina-san? Mano-a-mano, at that?!"

"Huh? Uh, yeah... Um, your eyes are popping out."

"Of course they are! Momohina-san's crazy strong! It's a wonder you're still alive, you know?!"

"She went easy on me," Haruhiro admitted.

"I'll bet! If not, you'd be a pile of fish bones right now. Oh, in the village I was born in, it's customary to sink corpses into the lake for the fishes to eat, and then we catch those same fish and eat them. Isn't that gross? You think it's gross, right?"

"I'm not sure I'd be on board with that, no..."

"I know, right?! I always thought it was gross. Either way, that's where the fish bones saying comes from, is what I'm getting at. That's some trivial knowledge for you. Trivia. You're sure you don't need to take notes?"

"I'll be fine."

"Oh, you kidder. It might do you some good to jot it down, you know? Or are you one of those people who thinks anything you forget was unimportant, but you'll remember the important things? Well, you'll forget a lot of the important things, too! Too bad!"

...Oh, crap.

Haruhiro wanted to sneak up behind this sahuagin, or whatever he was, and wring his neck right now. He didn't know how their bodies were built, but there was almost definitely going to be a vital nerve in the neck. If he could quickly deal a large amount of damage to it, he suspected the result would be deeply satisfying. Haruhiro had a lot of practice with that one idiot, so he figured he had more tolerance for annoying nonsense than the average person, but Ginzy had an inhuman level of annoyingness. Maybe because he was a fishman?

"I'm sorry," Haruhiro interrupted. "May I ask a question?"

"Yes, yes. If you must. If I can answer it, well, maybe I will? I don't know, though... You are new, after all, and just an underling, too."

"Oh...forget it, then."

"Ask! You're supposed to ask! You're still young, right?! I'm young, too, but the world's not so easy that you can get by with that level of enthusiasm, you know?!"

"No, I kinda forgot my question. Like, it doesn't even matter to me."

"Fishhhh!" Ginzy cried, bending over backwards like a shrimp... even though he was a fish, not a shrimp. Though, if Haruhiro said that, that would probably only encourage this fishman to keep going.

"Are all sahuagin, how should I put this...smooth talkers, like you?" he asked.

"Why, yes, we are. Why?"

"Oh, yeah? I see. I've never met a sahuagin before."

"Just kiddiiiing!"

"Huh?"

"That's a liiiiie! I'm more talkative than your average sahua-gin! Nyah nyah, I tricked you. Fishhhh! Fishhhh!"

Haruhiro wanted to commend himself for not pulling a Spider on Ginzy, who was repeatedly bending over backwards in shock, and eliminating a source of stress for himself.

The dinghy made several trips back and forth between the rocky beach and Ginzy's ship the *Mantis-go*. Once everyone was aboard the *Mantis-go,* they hoisted her sails and raised the anchor.

Their course was eastward and a little southward, in the direction of the Emerald Archipelago. Well, Haruhiro and his party weren't heading for there, but now that they were aboard the ship, they had bigger concerns.

Yes. Seasickness.

Haruhiro and company lined up along the side of the ship, battling with nausea, puking, and then battling with nausea again. When they rolled over in exhaustion to try to get some sleep, the pirates stopped them. If they laid down, they would be fine while they slept, but it would apparently be even worse once they woke up. The appropriate thing to do was drink some water with lime in it, and try to deal with it. That, and to avoid looking down. If they could just do that, they'd get used to eventually, they were told, but was that true? It was hard to believe, you know?

"Well, I've never heard of anyone dying of nausea," Jimmy the bandaged man told them. He would occasionally come to check on Haruhiro and the party. Of all the pirates, he might have been the most decent and normal. "This is something everyone, even those far weaker than you, has been through. You'll get through it somehow. Though, that said, I've never been seasick myself, so I don't really know what it's like."

"So some people don't get seasick," Haruhiro managed. "Is it a matter of constitution?"

"Well, I couldn't say. I'm an undead, so I don't really understand how you people who are properly alive feel."

"...Oh. I suppose you wouldn't, no."

Outside of his eyes and mouth, hardly any part of Jimmy was exposed. Not just his face; his neck, hands, and even his fingers were wrapped in cloth. Most undead had dirty-brown skin. Was it to hide that? But this pirate gang had orcs and goblins, so it wouldn't be that strange for an undead to be in it. Besides, Jimmy had told them he was undead on his own. It made no sense. Something was up with Jimmy, for sure.

Yume adapted in about half a day, and set out on a tour of the ship with Kiichi in tow. She apparently went for kung-fu lessons with Momohina, too.

Haruhiro, Kuzaku, Shihoru, Merry, and Setora never quite managed to get away from the side of the ship. Of course, it wasn't like they were constantly puking; they could talk, at least. It felt like conversation made it easier, but when one of them got sick, the others were dragged along. They were never going to get much talking done in this state.

"You'll never be proper pirates like that, you knooooow? Nope!" Momohina laughed at them.

Haruhiro agreed entirely, and wished she'd just let them

off the ship already. That it wasn't possible to do so was the scariest thing about a ship. On the high seas, there was no place to run.

Maybe it was because, in spite of the fair weather, the waves were high, and the boat rocked heavily. In the end, three days after they set sail, when an island appeared on the horizon, no one other than Yume and Kiichi had been completely set free from the nauseating grip of seasickness.

Once a sense of relief set in, though, their symptoms lessened a little, so there may have been more of a psychological aspect to it than they had thought.

However, when they got close to the island, it became apparent something strange was going on.

Ginzy's *Mantis-go* was headed for a port built in the island's bay. There were a whole bunch of ships outside the bay. It was a port, after all, and it wasn't evening yet. If there were a lot of ships going in and out, that would be understandable. However, there were more ships that had stopped than were moving. The crew of the *Mantis-go* was clearly on edge.

The figurehead of this ship, as the name would suggest, was a statue of a praying mantis. Momohina had been standing atop the figurehead for a while now, not moving a muscle. Her eyes were on the port. It would be scary if she fell off, but knowing Momohina, she probably wasn't even scared.

Haruhiro and the party were, as before, at the side of the ship. Jimmy happened to have come by at that moment, so they tried asking him what was happening, but he answered, "It'd be faster for you to see it, I think," and pointed towards the port.

"A bird?" Haruhiro cocked his head to the side. There were bird-like creatures circling over the port. A flock of two, maybe three birds. It looked like three. Was "flock" the right word? They were flying, so they weren't a herd, at least.

"But—"

"Kind of big, aren't they?" Yume said.

That was it. They were awfully big for birds.

"Wyverns?" Setora whispered. That made sense.

True enough, they did resemble the wyverns that lived in the Kuaron Mountains and descended on Thousand Valley when the fog cleared.

"Dragons have livedin the Emerald Archipelago since long, long ago," someone said.

If Jimmy had said that, it would have ended with an *Oh, okay.* But it wasn't Jimmy who said it.

Everyone there, not just Haruhiro, turned to look at Merry.

Why did Merry know that?

Merry covered her mouth and looked down, but Haruhiro was the one who was even more flustered.

"Ohh, that," said Haruhiro. "Um, like, I've heard that, too. It's just something we heard somewhere, so it's like, oh, yeah, that's a thing..."

"Ahhh!" Shihoru said in an awfully loud voice. Was she covering for them? No, not necessarily. The pirates were making a ruckus, too.

One of the dragons said to have lived in the Emerald

Archipelago since long, long ago had begun descending. If they were dragons, it seemed more fitting to call them a flight than a flock, and one of the three members of said flight had its head facing almost straight down as it descended, or rather fell.

The dragon reached the port, or probably the town beyond it, in no time flat, but what happened after that? It was far away, so it was impossible to tell from here.

"So, basically..." Haruhiro followed the two circling dragons with his eyes as he forced out a sigh.

It was happening again. One of the other two began a rapid descent. Then, the final one joined them.

Dust was rising from the town.

He had already been at a loss for what to do when they'd gotten shanghaied into joining a pirate crew. The boat trip had been the worst ever. Now, finally they were about to make landfall. Or so he had been thinking, but then this.

"...the port is under attack by dragons?"

Grimgar
of
Fantasy and Ash

7 | Jewels and Skulls

THE FLIGHT OF DRAGONS left in the evening. The *Mantis-go* entered port after that, so by the time they had disembarked and left the pier, it was quite late in the day.

It turned out the dragons had begun appearing ten days ago, and started swooping down like that seven days ago.

The damages extended to the port town of Roronea's residential district, commercial district, and pleasure quarter. The port had only had one of its piers destroyed, and two of the ships there were heavily damaged. Well, even if that was all that had happened, it still meant one of seven wharves and piers was completely out of commission. The ships were a major asset for their owners, too. Sometimes the entirety of their fortune. It was a huge loss.

That being the case, there were far fewer people in Roronea than usual. Normally, it would have been a wild town with drinking and singing all day and all night, a sort of sleepless city, but none of that bustle was on display now.

"Our company's main racket is the various taxes we collect from all over Roronea, after all," a man told them.

The man was sitting at a desk, looking out an open window. He wasn't quite middle age, but he gave off the impression of a mature man. His sailor style outfit suited him well, and he came off as far more captainly than either Momohina or Ginzy.

The mansion Momohina and the rest had been brought to stood on high ground, and the window of this second-floor room gave a full view of the port. The damp sea breeze felt lukewarm. There were a large number of moths in the room, perhaps drawn by the lamps inside, and they were fluttering around near the ceiling.

"The residences are one thing, but we have to pay to repair the pier ourselves," the man went on. "At this rate, we're going to be put out of business. I'd never have expected this nonsense would happen while the president and Kisaragi were away. Bad luck, that's what it is."

"No, this isn't the time for your luck nonsense," the fishman shot back. "You're the managing director!"

The man who'd been called the managing director seemed like he couldn't care less about Ginzy's objection. Ignoring the noisy sahuagin, he turned a scrutinizing eye on Haruhiro and the party.

"Newcomers, huh? It's not the sea. You people smell of the land. Were you volunteer soldiers from Alterna or something?"

Haruhiro didn't respond immediately. His comrades didn't open their mouths, either.

"Hey." The man cleared his throat and laughed. "I'm asking

you a question, you know? Answer it. You haven't trained them very well, have you, KMW?"

"Umm, I taught the girls kung-fu!"

"Did you, now?"

"Shihoruru's kind of iffy, but the other three maaay end up being pretty strong."

"Well, that's fine. Better than them being weak, I suppose."

"Hey, listen, do you think Yume can get stronger?" Yume asked suddenly.

Momohina let out a weird giggle and nodded. "You sure caaaan. I think you may be on the right track already, Yumeyume! If I train you good and hard for three, four months, you'll be an honest-to-goodness kung-fulier! Yep!"

"Oh-ho! Yume's gonna be a kung-fulier, huh?"

"Yumeyume, you're a hunter, riiiight? Your moves are a little more agile than the warriors, so maaaaybe that helps?"

"Hmmm. Yume's not stiff. Maybe Yume's pretty flexible?"

"Oh, and Harupiroron's a thief, Kuzakkyun's a paladin, and Shihoruru's a mage, right? Merimeri's, hmm, a priest, I think, but maaaaybe she's got experience in other classes, too. Setoranran's from the hidden village, I gueeeess? She's got a nyaa-chan with her, after all!"

"More or less volunteer soldiers, then." The managing director stroked his chin. "Well, maybe they'll be more use than dyed-in-the-wool pirates."

"Me, too! Me, too! Me, too! I'm not a pure pirate, either, after all!" Ginzy added proudly.

The managing director ignored him again. "Even our KMW, Momohina, was a volunteer soldier originally."

"Only a trainee, though," said Momohina. "Same with Kisaragicchon and Icchonchon."

"Now she's a head of a crew of pirates. That's life for you."

"And you're a pirate managing director, Giancarulun."

"Of a pirate company, yes. Though, when I get called that, even I don't really know what it means."

"The managing director! That's a kind of important person!"

"Dammiiiiit," Ginzy moaned. "I've been around longer, yet they only made me a captaiiiiin."

Momohina and the managing director, who was apparently named Giancarulun or something like that, didn't so much as look at Ginzy as he ground his teeth in frustration.

It wouldn't have been odd to feel a bit sorry for him, but there was something about this sahuagin that didn't produce the slightest bit of sympathy. That something was how annoying he was. Way too annoying.

"Come to think of it, I hadn't introduced myself yet," the managing director said with a shrug. "I'm technically the managing director of the K&K Pirate Company, Giancarlo Kreitzal."

"It's a pleasure. I'm Haruhiro."

Haruhiro greeted him as the party representative. However, he felt it strange the whole time. Why were they, the new recruits, being taken to meet an important executive of the pirate company?

That executive, Giancarlo, had this vague attitude of, *What the hell am I doing? Well, whatever. There are dragons. Everything's a mess.* He seemed disinterested, and listless.

Jimmy the bandaged man, who had remained quiet up until this point, stepped forward, whispering something in Giancarlo's ear. Giancarlo reacted like he finally got it, and nodded.

"Haruhiro, was it? Whatever led you here, you are now members of our K&K Pirate Company. Congratulations on joining the company. Okay, time to clap."

When Giancarlo started clapping, Momohina said, "Yay, clap, clap," saying the onomatopoeia out loud, while Jimmy clapped in silence. Who did Ginzy, who was clapping both his hands together while giving off an air of reluctance, think he was? Well, a captain, maybe.

It seemed like a rather forced celebration, but it didn't feel half bad.

Yeah, right.

Unfortunately, unlike Kuzaku, who scratched the back of his head in embarrassment with an "Uhh, thanks..." or Yume, who bowed politely with a "Thank youuuu," Haruhiro was not so pure and innocent.

He quickly traded glances with Shihoru. Shihoru, like Haruhiro, was dubious. From the looks on their faces, Setora and Merry were suspicious, too. When it came to Kiichi, who was sticking close to Setora's feet, he'd been in alert mode from the beginning.

"By the way, sorry if this is an awkward question, but, um... what sort of organization is the K&K Pirate Company, exactly?" Haruhiro asked. "If we've 'joined' the company, I think you could tell us that much, at least."

"Huh? You weren't told?" Giancarlo spat the words out in exasperation, then looked to Jimmy and made a gesture with his chin.

Jimmy nodded, turning back to Haruhiro. "The Emerald Archipelago was originally run by this big pirate called Dead Skull."

According to him, the Emerald Archipelago had long been called a pirate's paradise. It had ports where pirates with nowhere else to go could stop safely, and was a place for them to rest their weary bones. Some pirates had been born in the Emerald Archipelago, too. There were even rumors that the islands were the birthplace of piracy.

However, when the Skull Pirate Gang under Dead Skull had taken the place over, the Emerald Archipelago had ceased to be a paradise for many of those pirates.

Thought of as a man of character, an understanding and moderate pirate captain, Skull had been a large man, with white hair and a white beard.

When he had first come to the Emerald Archipelago, he'd called himself an old man. His underlings had called Skull "Old Man."

Good at arbitrating when there was trouble and acting as a middleman, there had been a continuous series of people who brought profitable ideas to the old man, and made a fortune working with him. The old man had connections in trading cities like Vele and Igor, in the Coral Archipelago, and on the Red Continent, too.

Whenever a pirate had consulted him about something, the old man had always started with, "I'm just an old man. I don't know if I can help you," but then handled it or provided a plan of action.

Quickly becoming acquainted with the top pirates, the old man had in no time gained a role as a coordinator.

Then, one day, he had shown his true colors.

On his seventy-seventh birthday, he had told the other pirates he'd like to share a drink before he passed on.

With each pirate thinking he would be drinking with the old man alone at the tavern, all the biggest names in piracy had gathered in the Emerald Archipelago.

Fair enough; this was apparently what the old man wanted. A birthday party, huh?

There were pirates forced to sit with those they didn't get along with, but how could they complain? Having decided to help the old man look good, and to put up with one another for the night, they had all shared a toast.

That was the last drink any of them had ever taken.

The pirates had dropped like flies. The booze had been poisoned.

The old man had tricked the powerful pirates and done away with them, becoming dictator of the Emerald Islands in a single night.

Anyone who refused to swear loyalty to Dead Skull had been captured by the Skull Pirate Gang and executed. Men and women alike. Even a twelve-year-old girl had been killed for bad-mouthing Skull.

Their standard modus operandi was incredibly cruel, cutting off the nose and ears, then throwing the victims into the sea for the sharks to eat.

Despite shuddering, everyone had understood that there was no choice but to submit to Skull.

"And who brought down Dead Skull?" Ginzy declared, his nostrils flaring. "I...am good friends with Kisaragi-san, who, along with his comrades, did the deed!"

"K&K is short for Kisaragi and Kreitzal." Jimmy's tone was plain. Naturally, he didn't even look at Ginzy. "Kisaragi didn't want a post with the company, so Giancarlo's younger sister, Anjolina, is our company president. She was a pirate to begin with, and opposed the Skull Pirate Gang."

Giancarlo smiled wryly. "I, well, I'm riding the coattails of Kisaragi and my little sister. Not that I particularly wanted this job."

"Where are this Kisaragi and Anjolina now?" Haruhiro asked.

Momohina jumped up. "Um, well, they're reeeeally, reaaaally far away!" she explained energetically. "Kisaragicchon, Icchonchon, Miriryun, and Haimari got on Ms. President's boat and left for the Red Continent. Ms. President's on a business triiiip! That's right!"

"Oh, and Mitsuki's probably not coming back," Giancarlo added with a sigh. "Still, Momohina, why didn't you go with Kisaragi? You've never been to the Red Continent, right? It may not be a nice place, but it's worth seeing."

"Hmmm..." Momohina looked up to the moths flying around near the ceiling. "Kisaragicchon has Icchonchon, Miriryun, and Haimari with him, so I figured he'll be fiiiine. If you love someone, let them goooo. Ooooh. You know? Like that?"

"Nyuk nyuk nyuk..." Ginzy laughed creepily. "Love is complicated, isn't it? How nice. Oh, such youth! Why, I've never ever been popular with the ladies! Lately, I've been thinking of giving up on sahuagin women, and setting my sights on humans instead! Oh, oh, oh, oh, what's this? No witty retorts? I welcome those, you know! Come on, come on, come on, tell me, tell me I'll have even less luck with humans! Three, two, one, go!"

It was quiet.

About the only noises to be heard were the distant waves, and the wings of moths beating against the ceiling.

It wasn't as if anyone had taken the lead on this, but there was an unspoken understanding that no one would take this sahuagin's bait. In a way, Ginzy had brought them all together on something, so that was kind of amazing.

"Dragons have lived in the Emerald Archipelago since long, long ago," Jimmy said.

Merry stiffened a little. Those were the exact words Merry had spoken while the dragons were attacking Roronea. "But the pirates of the Emerald Archipelago have always coexisted with the dragons. There was an unspoken understanding: 'Don't go near the dragons.' Trying to harm them is, obviously, out of the question. The dragons are like seabirds, feeding on large fish. Not far from this island, there's a perfect fishing spot for dragons.

We never disturb that fishing spot. As long as pirates just followed these rules, the dragons have left them be. As an added bonus, respectable ships feared the dragons, and they wouldn't come near the Emerald Archipelago. The dragons were almost like protector gods for the pirates."

"Isn't that weird?" Setora asked in a tone too bold for a newcomer and an underling. She might simply have no concept of acting servile. "Why are those protector gods attacking the town?"

Jimmy didn't seem offended. "Yes, it is weird," he agreed. "Managing director, how is that investigation going?"

"We're trying to investigate, but..." Giancarlo frowned. "I have my usual duties, and I can be pretty busy with them, and then the dragons make more work for me each time they come. The only pawns I have at my disposal are a bunch of ruffians. Jimmy, if I had a clever guy like you, I might make some progress."

"That's an excuse!" Ginzy shouted.

"Hey, shut up, Ginzy. You wanna get cooked and then thrown out?"

"Fishhh?! I didn't get ignored, for once?! I'm kind of happy! But isn't cooking me then throwing me out without eating me a little harsh?!"

"I understand." Jimmy completely ignored the fishman. "I'm tired of riding on ships, getting shipwrecked, and waiting to be rescued, so let me take this on for you. I am a section head, after all."

"What section are you the head of?" Shihoru asked.

Jimmy said, "Search me," and tilted his head to the side a bit. "I was asked to choose between assistant director, section head, and department head, and just went with whatever, so I don't even know. When I'm on a ship, I'm more important than the rest of the crew, but less important than the captain. On land I'm above the captains, but below the managing director. That's about how the company's structured. So, about that investigation, I'm going to need people."

Giancarlo waved his hand as if to say, *Do whatever you want,* then glanced to Haruhiro.

"Why, isn't this convenient," Jimmy began.

I see where this is going, thought Haruhiro.

Haruhiro made his move before Jimmy could bring it up. "Sure. We'll help. I'm sure we'll be a little more useful than the pirates. There's a condition, though."

Grimgar
of
Fantasy and Ash

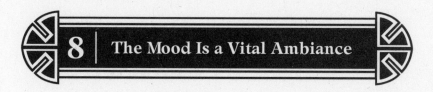

8 | The Mood Is a Vital Ambiance

A LONG TIME AGO, it had felt burdensome to even just haggle over prices in Alterna's shops. Now Haruhiro was launching negotiations himself like it was totally natural, and trying to get the best compromise he could out of the other side.

He wasn't one to boast, but he felt like he'd gotten a whole lot bolder.

Haruhiro's initial condition was that they be allowed to quit being pirates, or in other words to be dismissed from the K&K Pirate Company, and then to form a new limited contract for the investigation of the Roronea Dragon Attacks Incident.

After all, Haruhiro and his group had discovered the entrance to that unknown underground world, the Dusk Realm, in the Wonder Hole. In addition, they had wandered from the Dusk Realm into Darunggar, climbed up Fire Dragon Mountain from the orc town of Waluandin, and after many difficulties returned to Grimgar.

Then, after making it out of dangerous Thousand Valley somehow and going through various events, they had crossed the sea to arrive here, in the Emerald Archipelago.

Not many people had as much experience as they had. Looking at their career history, they were less like volunteer soldiers and more like a group of professional adventurers.

So, if they were going to investigate the dragons as adventurers, they weren't unwilling to accept the job. However, if the company wanted professionals to do a professional job, they deserved to be treated like professionals.

Managing Director Giancarlo seemed ready to accept, but Ginzy stubbornly refused. The pirates had their own rules, including one which stated that a captain was elected by his crew, and if one of those crew members had a request, the captain approved or rejected it. If a crew member didn't like that, the proper thing to do was to challenge the captain to a duel.

"Momohina-san made you her underlings, so if you want out, you should tell that to Momohina-san!" Ginzy shouted. "Not that she'll let you! Right, Momohina-san?! I'm right, aren't I?!"

"Hmm. That's right. Harupiroron and his friends aaaare my underlings, after all."

"See! See, see, see! There you have it! There's only one method left for you people! Duel Momohina-san! Win, and you're free and clear to quit being pirates!"

No, Haruhiro couldn't win. If he could have won, he wouldn't have become a pirate in the first place.

In the end, he kept haggling, and the deal they ultimately settled on was that Haruhiro and the party would investigate as members of the K&K Pirate Company, in other words still as pirates, but if they discovered the cause of the attacks, they would be rewarded.

There were two rewards. The first was to quit being pirates. The second was that they would be brought to the free city of Vele by ship.

If they made it to Vele as free people, Alterna would suddenly be a lot closer.

The first thing Haruhiro and his group did was view the places the dragons had attacked.

"This is the pier destroyed by the dragons, huh?" Haruhiro mused.

The dragons had first come ten days ago. The next day, and the day after that, they had only flown around in the air above Roronea.

Then, seven days ago, before noon, the first attack had happened on this No. 2 Pier.

They had left the mansion immediately after the end of the negotiations, so it was still night. The dragons would start flying once it was light out, so the party had to act in darkness. They were pretty worn out by their voyage, or rather the accompanying sea sickness, but, well, it wasn't going to kill them.

The No. 2 Pier had apparently been in the shape of the letter F. Haruhiro crouched and lit up the area at their feet with his lamp.

The sea was below. This was what would have been the bottom of the F's horizontal line. Had the dragons landed here?

The bridge planks were crushed, of course, and the girders were, too. It looked like a number of the support pillars were broken, as well.

"How is it?" Merry crouched down next to him, brushing her hair back behind her ear.

"Mmm..." Haruhiro mumbled an appropriate response like, "It's bad," or something similar.

In light of the fact that the damage done by the dragons was spread over a wide area, the party had decided to split up. Haruhiro and Merry were at Pier No. 2.

He hadn't needed a guide to find the port, and only one pier had been destroyed, so he'd been able to figure out where it was quickly.

Haruhiro would have been fine by himself, but if Setora and Kiichi were counted as one unit, there were six of them, so they had split into three pairs of two. He would have been fine with anyone as his partner, but for some reason Shihoru and Yume and Kuzaku and Setora had quickly formed pairs, leaving him with Merry.

That, in itself, was no problem whatsoever. But...

"This must be where the ships were destroyed, too." Merry was her usual self. Or she looked it, at least.

Haruhiro needed to maintain his composure, too, though that wasn't the reason why. "Looks like it. The two ships moored to this pier were taken out. But from what we heard, the piers and wharves haven't been attacked since, right?"

"So it's like they were after the ships, maybe?"

"Ever since they took out this No. 2 Pier, the ships have stopped coming into port during the day. The dragons aren't attacking the piers and wharves because they don't see any ships. Hmm, but if that were the case, they'd attack the ships taking shelter outside the port, wouldn't they?"

"You could be right. If so, could it have just been coincidence that this pier and the ships were the first things destroyed?"

"It could be...or it could not. We can't say anything just yet. But it's interesting that they only hit the port once."

Haruhiro rested his lamp on the bridge planks. He took a breath.

He wanted to know more about the dragons. He'd asked Jimmy, of course, but it turned out even the pirates based out of the Emerald Archipelago didn't know a whole lot about the dragons. In fact, the pirates' basic attitude towards the issue was that it was better not to know about dragons, and they didn't need to.

Up until now, the pirates and dragons had gotten along well enough by not interacting or interfering with one another. Why had that relationship broken down now?

"The cause can't be the dragons," Haruhiro said. "I'm sure the humans did something first."

"I agree."

"The dragons aren't attacking Roronea to eat the pirates, or anything like that. I hear the dragons are still fishing in their usual spot."

"Did someone do something to make the dragons angry, maybe?"

"But if that were the problem, I feel like the dragons could've trashed this place a whole lot worse..."

"Sorry," Merry said.

"Huh?"

"I wish I knew more that could help." Merry hung her head as if trying to rub her face into her knees.

It would be easy to say, *Don't worry about it.* But how could she not? This probably had to do with Merry's, how to put this— Merry's personal problem. If it had been something external to her, it would've been easy to turn a blind eye to it, but for a problem that was internal to herself, she couldn't do that.

I'm happy to lend an ear, Haruhiro thought. *Why don't you tell me about it? I mean, just getting it out there might make you feel a little better. No matter what you say, I'll be fine. You don't have to worry about that.*

Any number of words came to mind. They all sounded cheap, insincere, or off base, so it was hard to say them.

What if, rather than talking to her, he just hugged her tight?

No, that was just what he wanted to do, wasn't it? Wouldn't that be taking advantage of her weakness? Still, Merry was probably feeling weak right now. He wanted to encourage her. Cheering her up couldn't be a bad thing. No, no, but how did that lead to him hugging her, or anything like that?

How much of it was him thinking about Merry, and how much of it was just his own desires?

Honestly, he wished he could just cut it all away. To think only of Merry. If he could not worry about himself, and think for Merry's sake, and only for her sake, how much better would that be?

It made Haruhiro realize it all over again. That he loved Merry.

It was out of love that he wanted to make his love for her go away. He wished he could fully erase his own feelings, so he could make a proper decision about what was best for Merry. Thoughts about how he wanted to touch her, or how he wanted to do this or that, or how it would be nice if things turned out a certain way, popped up one after another, and he couldn't banish them. He wished that part of him would just die.

"There should be someone who knows about the dragons somewhere." Merry raised her face, looked at Haruhiro, and smiled. "This may be a pirate's paradise, but there are more than just pirates on this island. The original residents are here, too…I think."

"That makes sense." Haruhiro hid how confused he was, picking up the lamp as he stood.

This was the Emerald Archipelago. There were a number of islands. The odds were good there were natives around somewhere.

Even without knowing that, he could more or less guess. That was right. Even if she didn't know…

If that one insensitive jerk were around, he'd probably say, *What's it matter? If she knows things she couldn't possible know, and uses magic she couldn't possibly use, that's just convenient.*

Was it all right to take it lightly like that? If they did, Merry might not have to worry. Haruhiro wouldn't say that, though, "What's it matter?" That would be a little too much.

Haruhiro and Merry met up with Team Yume and Team Kuzaku before dawn. They figured if they got away from the town for now, the odds of avoiding being victims of a dragon attack were high.

They sorted through the information they had so far on the beach outside Roronea with Section Head Jimmy of the K&K Pirate Company.

It was a new day, so the first day of the dragon attacks had now been eight days ago. Only one dragon had come, destroying the No. 2 Pier, heavily damaging two ships, and causing around thirty casualties.

Seven days ago, another dragon had come, attacking the pleasure quarter, leveling three drinking establishments, and only injuring twenty people, no deaths. Probably because not many people went drinking in the middle of the day.

Six days ago, two dragons had descended on the commercial district, where the marketplace and stores were concentrated, and the damage had been much, much greater. More than ten dead, and over a hundred injured.

Starting five days ago, two dragons had gone to smash homes in the residential district for three days in a row. More than twenty houses were now wholly or partially destroyed. The dead and wounded numbered over fifty.

The day before yesterday, a third dragon had appeared for the first time. On that day, two bars in the pleasure quarter and ten homes in the residential district had been damaged. Apparently not too many casualties.

Finally, yesterday, there had been three dragons again. Eight residences had been demolished, and the marketplace was almost wholly ruined. However, everyone but the elderly had evacuated, so there were few casualties from that attack.

The dragons would come flying once the sun had fully risen. They wouldn't circle over Roronea the whole time; they would wander off to their fishing grounds, too. If they followed the same pattern, they would attack the town just once or twice a day, heading home before the sun set.

It seemed the pirates really didn't know much about the dragons.

The Emerald Archipelago was made up of the main island, Emerald Island; three islands to the east of it, Kunu Island, Rema Island, and Hosu Island; and then a number of smaller islands. The dragons lived in a place on the north of the main island called Dragon's Nest, and Roronea was on a bay at the southern end.

The dragons' fishing grounds were an area of sea that was two or three kilometers southeast of Roronea. From Roronea, the dragons could be spotted flying there on practically a daily basis. Everyone was aware that there were multiple dragons. However, nobody knew precisely how many of them there were.

The dragons that lived on this island had scales like emeralds. That was apparently where the name Emerald Island had come from. They were winged and flew. They caught and ate fish at their fishing grounds.

In terms of size, some were about thirty meters with their wings spread. There was individual variance, though. The larger dragons were older, and the smaller ones were presumably younger. Maybe they were parents and their children.

That was about all the pirates knew about the dragons.

Soon enough, the sun came up. The three dragons flew in and began circling over Roronea.

"Can't we kill them?" Setora asked.

"Oh, I've wondered that, too." Kuzaku was sitting on the beach with his long legs spread wide. Seeing as Kiichi was curled up using those legs as a pillow, the nyaa might be sleeping. When had they started getting along? "It's three that come to attack the town, right? I get the feeling that if we could take out just the big one, they might stop coming, maybe."

"You'd be in the most danger, you know that, right, Kuzaku-kun?" Shihoru asked.

"Well, yeah," Kuzaku replied, screwing up his face and raising just one of his eyebrows. "Like, if I can keep it still, couldn't everyone else handle the rest?"

"That's too haphazard..." Merry muttered.

"No, if we seriously decide to do it, I'll think if over properly, okay? I dunno. It's a question of choices, you could say. I was wondering if defeating the dragons is an option."

Haruhiro frowned. "I'd rather not take risks we don't have to..."

Yume mimed firing an arrow from her bow. "Do you think arrows'd work?"

"Their scales are too hard for arrows to pierce," was Jimmy's answer to that. "Just so you're aware, the brave, stupid pirates who tried firing on them with crossbows all died. I don't know about magic. If you want to try it, be my guest. I won't stop you."

"Guns?" Haruhiro asked, but Jimmy shook his head a little.

"Kisaragi and the others who went to the Red Continent have a number of them, but we have only one left in our possession. That, and there's no gun powder. As far as I'm aware, the shot we fired to intimidate you people used up the last of it."

Even if they'd had the gunpowder for it, just one gun wasn't going to be able to do anything. No, multiple guns wouldn't change things. If the dragons were flying, they probably couldn't hit them.

"Then do you know anyone familiar with the dragons?" Haruhiro asked. "Pirate or otherwise."

Jimmy thought for a moment before opening his mouth. "I have an idea. There are people who lived on this island before the pirates built Roronea. They're from a race called runarukas, though."

The natives of Emerald Island, runarukas, lived in the forested areas of the main island, and on Rema Island, Hosu Island, and a number of the smaller islands. The runarukas, like the dragons, were a mysterious race, and nearly nothing was known about them for certain. However, they didn't oppose the pirates, and they had trade relations with them. Rarely a young runaruka would come into Roronea, and there were even times when they became pirates.

"Our company has one runaruka pirate, actually," Jimmy said. "But they can barely use the common human language we're speaking in now. They don't speak the orcish language or undead Manguish, either. The runarukas are secretive by nature, so I don't know if they could be any help. They may not be much use."

Whatever the case, they would have to meet that crew member and talk first. When Haruhiro asked him to do so, Jimmy agreed, and at a little past noon, he brought that runaruka to the beach.

They were just about to start with the introductions when the dragons began descending on Roronea.

"Ahh. Etwa, unakai, nye, shatah..." The runaruka spoke what sounded like words, covering their chest with both hands and shaking their head.

It wasn't clear if it was male or female. To put it plainly, it looked like a fox. Its face was fox-like, at the very least. It wore sailor's clothing. Its body was similar to a bipedal human or orc's, but the arms were relatively short in relation to the torso. Its whole body was covered in fur. There was a hole in the butt of its pants, and a tail sticking out through it.

One dragon descended to Roronea, and dust and smoke began to rise. The remaining two were still up in the sky.

"Nyarah, nyarah..." Was the runaruka lamenting, or fearful?

"Yeah, killing them's probably out of the question..." Kuzaku said.

The runaruka went, "Hah!" with eyes open wide. "Kill? Nah. Kill. Nah! Dorahga, etwana, vitwa, she, gwadwa."

"No, I have no clue what you're saying..."

"Kill, dorahga, nah!"

"Y'think it's sayin' that killin' the dragons'd be bad?" Yume asked.

"Huh? Yume-san, you understand what this person's saying?" Kuzaku answered.

"Hmm. Not understand, so much as have a feelin' for it? Maybe?"

"Kill, dorahga, nah!" The runaruka turned to Yume and repeated with a nod. "Kill, nah! Dragon. Dorahga. Kill, good, not."

According to Yume's feeling translation, the runaruka's name was Tsiha, and it was somewhere in between a man and a woman. Runaruka children chose whether they would be a man or a woman when they grew up. Tsiha had yet to choose either, but was not a child anymore, so that put it somewhere between a man and a woman.

Runarukas had been living on Emerald Island since long, long ago. Then a male dorahga and female dorahga—or, in other words, a mating pair of dragons—had come to the island. The lives of the runarukas had improved ever since, so they saw the dorahgas as messengers from God.

There had been a number of times in past when the runarukas had done something bad and angered the dorahgas. Tsiha wouldn't go into the details, because if Tsiha mentioned anything frightening, something called a gewguw would appear and would make Tsiha sick. Gewguw were dark black in color, and would sneak in under cover of darkness, so they couldn't be seen. However, when a gewguw was near, a chill wind would blow, so

113

you could immediately tell, Tsiah said. It seemed the secretiveness of the runarukas had to do with these gewguws.

Haruhiro happened to agree when Tsiha said that someone had done something wrong, and that had enraged the dorahgas. If the runarukas had done it, the dorahgas would have attacked the forests where the runarukas lived. So if Roronea was being attacked, it surely meant the pirates had done something they shouldn't have.

"Bad! Dorahga! Angry! Grrr! What? Grrr!" Yume cried. "What make dorahga grrr? Angry?"

Yume tried a number of times, working pantomime into her questions, but Tsiha kept mum and wouldn't say, they assumed because Tsiha was afraid of the gewguw.

The three dragons went on a rampage in Roronea, then took off and began circling again.

The vast majority of the populace now expected the dragons would come, so they avoided the streets during the day. There were some who stayed in town as a test of courage, and some drunkards who kept drinking in spite of it all, but probably no one had died. Though the damage to the buildings and roads was extensive, the dragons hadn't gotten serious. Well, there was no way to know how they actually felt, but it was clear they had to be holding back. If not, Roronea would be in more trouble, and much worse would have been done to the town. All of the pirates, the K&K Pirate Company included, would have long since fled the island.

However, that hadn't happened.

Why was that?

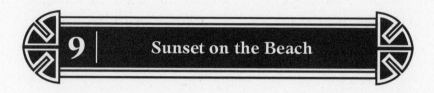

9 | Sunset on the Beach

THIS WAS KIND OF FUN.

He could hear them.

Voices, coming from somewhere.

That, and the sound of the waves.

He should open his eyes. That would be the best thing. But he didn't want to.

Naturally, he couldn't keep them closed forever. He knew that.

But just a little longer.

For just a little longer, he wanted to stay like this.

Basically, he was tired. Exhausted in body and soul. Of course he was. He hadn't been able to sleep properly on the boat, thanks to the sea sickness. Then, when they'd finally made landfall, they'd gotten caught up in something ridiculous again.

That was why. Yeah.

When the dragons had flown off earlier, he'd thought maybe he'd take a nap.

He felt like when night came, there would be things he had to do. He didn't really know anymore, though. He sensed his head had stopped working, like he was at his limit.

"Sorry, I'm gonna sleep for a bit," he'd said, and no one had objected.

Or so he thought. Probably. His memories were a little vague. He'd gone over to a place that seemed decent, then went to sleep.

It wasn't dark yet. Or maybe he'd slept all night, and the dawn had come. No, that wasn't possible. If so, he'd be more awake. He hadn't dreamed. Not that he remembered, at least. His mind was gradually getting clearer.

His feelings of, *Do I have to get up? I wanna lie around more,* and his will that said, *I've gotta get up,* were conflicting with one another.

Whew... He took a breath, and...

"Oh, did you wake up?" someone said to him.

"Yeah," he responded, sitting up at the same time as his eyes opened.

This beach faced onto the sea in the southwest. The setting sun was poking its face out from beyond the edge of the sea, illuminating the surface of the water. The western sky and sea both looked like they were on fire.

The breeze, which was so slight it only occasionally played with his hair a little, was as unpleasantly warm as ever. Before his night sweats could dry, he started to sweat again. If he said, *Whew, it's hot,* he felt like that would only make him feel hotter, so he made a point of not saying it. Well, it was better than it being cold, at least. Still, it was damn hot. That must have been why the girls were frolicking barefoot by the edge of the water.

No, not just the edge, they were in up to just below their knees.

"Sploooosh!" Yume scooped up a large volume of water in her hands, then splashed it in the direction of Shihoru, Merry, and Setora.

"Eek!" Shihoru screamed and clung to Merry.

Setora jumped back. "Hah!" She planted a sharp kick on the surface of the water.

"Meow!" Yume cried. Having taken a face full of seawater, she lunged at Setora. "Murrrrr!"

Setora nimbly danced away.

Yume cried, "Gotcha!" and ended up taking a shallow dive in the sea, but she was soon back up and clinging to Setora's right leg.

"Meowwwn!"

"Wait, you, sto—"

"Mrowwwww!"

"Owww!" Setora was dragged into the sea. The depth was maybe thirty centimeters, but it was more than enough to leave her fully drenched.

The two of them were soon rolling around in the water.

"Damn you, hunter! Stop! Let go!"

"Call Yume 'Yume'! If you do, then Yume'll let you go!"

"Who would call you that?!"

"If that's how you're gonna be, Yume's not lettin' go!"

"You stubborn...!"

Shihoru and Merry were smiling and watching the two of them tussle—or so it looked, until Merry suddenly went, "There!" and pushed Shihoru.

Shihoru cried, "Eek?!" and fell, getting soaking wet. "That was mean!"

As if to say, *I'm not going to let you get away with that,* Shihoru splashed Merry with seawater, too.

"It's salty!" Merry complained as she got back at her.

"Ha ha..." Haruhiro found it deeply funny. But at the same time, there was a heat in the back of his nose, and he pressed on the bridge of his nose despite himself.

Kuzaku sniffled. "I know it's weird to say this with what just happened to the town, but..."

Kuzaku had taken off his armor and was topless. Kiichi was lying against Kuzaku's legs with his eyes closed, but judging by the way his ears were perked up, the nyaa wasn't sleeping.

"It sure is peaceful, huh? When was the last time we relaxed like this?"

"I wonder."

It wasn't like they were on edge all the time. If they hadn't let their guards down here and there, they'd never have made it this far. But it was true, it didn't feel like there were many times when they'd been able to relax like this.

"It's like summer vacation," Haruhiro said.

"Ohh..." Kuzaku laughed a little, then wiped his forehead with his hand. "Summer vacation, huh...?" he murmured, then said, "Yeah," with a nod. It seemed to take him a while to find the next words to say. "Summer vacation, huh? Like, I know what that means. Somehow, this feels different. I can't explain it well. What summer vacation is, I mean. I...I wonder what's with me."

"I know, right?" Haruhiro said. "It's weird saying this when I'm the one who used those words, but I kind of get where you're coming from."

"But it really is summer vacation-y, right? This is nice."

"It sure is."

"But man, those girls sure are energetic, huh?"

"You're not tired, Kuzaku?"

"I was resting here, so I'm fine, sort of."

"Was I snoring?" Haruhiro ventured.

"Just a little."

"Whoa, seriously?"

"I think you were more beat than I was," Kuzaku said. "You use your head, after all."

"I hope I'm using it well."

"I'm not thinking at all. You're letting me take it easy there..." Kuzaku yawned, languidly moving his head from left to right.

There were what looked like logs scattered around on this sandy beach. Occasionally, they would move slowly. They weren't driftwood or anything like that. They were living creatures. They were like seals, but rounder. If you got close to them, they'd get really startled, but from a distance they were pretty darn cute.

Seeing those sort of sea-beast-like animals relaxing, and with so many of them lying around, might be one reason why their hearts were so at ease.

"Is it okay to get soaked with saltwater like that?" Haruhiro mused. "I feel like, unlike freshwater, it doesn't just dry..."

"Yeah." Kuzaku laughed. "They were only going to get their feet wet at first. Then Yume went in deep. At some point, all of them just stopped caring about that, I guess."

"They are awfully energetic, aren't they?" There was a sudden voice behind him, which surprised Haruhiro.

When he turned around, an undead wrapped in bandages, with clothes on over top of them, was crouching there.

"Oh..." Haruhiro said. "Section head. That's where you were. I didn't know."

"I'd been awake for a while, too, so I was resting."

"You weren't moving at all," Kuzaku said, then let out another light yawn.

Now Yume was attacking Merry. Maybe she had let her guard down, because Shihoru was tickling Setora's ribs.

"Come to think of it, do undead sleep, too?" Kuzaku's question felt maybe a little rude, but on second thought, maybe it wasn't.

"We sleep," Jimmy answered plainly. "Though I suspect our sleep is a little different from yours. You humans have dreams, right?"

"Sometimes we don't, though. Wait, undead don't dream?"

"Yeah. They say we have a long dream just before we're destroyed, but no one can really know that. Our sleep is... How should I express this? It's like everything's turned to sludge. As if we're drowning in a swamp."

"Sounds like that'd actually make you more tired," Haruhiro commented.

Jimmy checked the state of his bandages. "It's not a pleasant feeling, I'll give you that," he acknowledged. "But if we stay awake, that swamp presses in on us. We get sleepy, you could say. I think between pleasure and displeasure, we feel considerably more of the latter. In words you might use, we're not having a very fun time."

"Whoa," Kuzaku put in. "Guess I'm glad to be human, then."

Jimmy looked displeased. "Kuzaku, you..."

"Ah, sorry. It's not like Jimmy-san decided to be an undead."

"I didn't, no," Jimmy said without raising his voice and smiled. "I hate the undead. That includes myself, you know. What is a living being? I'd say it's one that grows, reproduces, and has life. In which case, we undead are not living creatures. Life is too abstract a concept for me to understand, but we don't grow, and we don't reproduce. What exactly are we, I wonder? It would be easier if we could just not think, like the hollow zombies and skeletons moving around under No-Life King's curse."

"You're a lot like a human, Jimmy-san," Kuzaku said. "No, not that I know what other undead are like."

"I'm pretending to be human, Kuzaku-kun. Even though, no matter what I do, I can't be human."

"Hmmm. I don't understand complicated things. But whether it's an act or not, if you look like the part, isn't that fine? Jimmy-san, you're doing it because you hate undead, and you'd prefer to be like a human, right? Setting aside the question of whether there's anything wrong with being undead, that's what you're doing."

"Yes... I wanted to become anything other than an undead, if I could. But it's impossible."

Kuzaku shook his head. "That, I dunno what to call it, that will? That's important. More than what race you are, I think that's the more important thing. What you want to do, and what you actually do. Honestly, I don't think it matters what race you are. I don't mind guys like you, Jimmy-san. Not that I know you all that well. But I get that sense."

"I see." Jimmy's tone was level. Even so, his emotions showed through subtly in intonation and gaps between words. Like now, for instance. "You're the second human to have said something like that to me. You must be a curious fellow, I'm sure."

Jimmy was probably happy. But at the same time, he might have felt embarrassed.

Kuzaku was a curious fellow. He was also a good guy.

Thinking about it, his first party had been wiped out, and Kuzaku had survived all by his lonesome. Despite that incredibly harsh experience, he'd crawled back up from the very bottom. On top of that, he hadn't waited for anyone to help him; he'd moved on his own. He had a positivity that Haruhiro lacked.

Kuzaku didn't have a tragic air about him, and wasn't cynical. Even when he'd had feelings for Merry and gotten rejected, he hadn't gotten depressed by it.

Wait, hold on. Why had Merry rejected Kuzaku? He was a pretty good guy, right? He was a real catch, wasn't he? Not like a fish, though. But, no, seriously.

If Haruhiro were a woman, and a guy like Kuzaku liked him,

well, he wouldn't feel bad about that. The way the guy acted like a youngest child made him feel a bit unreliable at times, but he still put his life on the line without hesitation. He tickled the maternal instincts, but at the same time, he was manly. He was such a good guy that, for a time, Haruhiro had been jealous of him. It made him sad to think how small-hearted he'd been.

"Mrrow?! Haru-kun's woken up!" Yume shouted.

He looked over.

"Nweeee!" Yume waved her arms wide.

Haruhiro waved back. "I just woke up."

"Well then, Haru-kun and Kuzakkun, why don't you come on over?! Jimmy-chan, too! Everyone can play together!"

"I'll pass," Jimmy said simply. "I can't swim."

"Huh? But you're a pirate..."

"Undead sink."

"They do?"

"That may only be me, though."

"Okay." Kuzaku shook his left leg and waited for Kiichi to move away on his own before standing up. "Let's go, Haruhiro. Every once in a while we need some...recreation? To deepen our bonds as comrades, you could say. That stuff's important."

"I guess..."

Haruhiro was still kind of exhausted and, truth be told, he was reluctant to do it, but he had to go with the flow here. Besides, it would probably be fun in its own way. With an "Oof," Haruhiro got up.

"Come on, run." Kuzaku pulled him by the arm.

"Whoa..." Haruhiro nearly tripped, and Kuzaku laughed.

It was too much hassle to complain about everything. Haruhiro picked up the pace and didn't resist.

"Oh, right, be careful." Jimmy was saying something.

"Huh, what?" Haruhiro tried to turn back, but Kuzaku lifted him up with a grunt and threw him into the sea. "Hey, wait, where'd this idiot strength come fro—"

The water was only up to their ankles here, but it was sand, so it was soft, and he managed to fall gracefully. Still, his whole body got wet.

Haruhiro jumped up. "What was that for?! Damn it, Kuzaku!"

"Wahahaha! Catch me if you caaaan!"

Kuzaku raised his leg awfully high, making large splashes as he took off running.

"Hold up!" Haruhiro chased after him.

Partly because of the strange way he was running, Kuzaku wasn't all that fast. Haruhiro would catch him in no time.

"Ha! You're wide open!" Yume cried as she jumped him from behind.

"You're too obvious!" Haruhiro sidestepped, dodging Yume's charge.

When Kuzaku did an about-face and went on the attack, too, Haruhiro predicted it.

"Here it comes! Body Slam...!"

"Who'd let that hit them?!" Haruhiro shouted.

He didn't go sideways, or backwards. Forwards. Haruhiro lowered his stance, passing underneath Kuzaku as he came at him with a tackle, both arms spread wide.

"Gwah!" Kuzaku ended up using his Body Slam, or whatever it was, on the seawater. Haruhiro paused to watch.

Maybe that was a mistake.

"You're mine!" From behind him, it was Setora's voice.

Haruhiro didn't turn, attempting to escape with a sideways jump. Was he too slow?

"The techniques of the onmitsu spies are also known as ninjutsu! Flying Windmill...!"

Haruhiro let out a gasp. What was this? He'd probably been grabbed by the back and thighs. Then what? He didn't know.

Whatever it was, Haruhiro's body spun around sideways with incredible momentum. Setora could use these sorts of physical techniques, too? And, hold on, it wasn't fair pulling out a technique like that here!

Haruhiro was pounded into the bottom of the shallow water. When he tried to get up, he was already surrounded by his comrades.

"Hey! Ah! Five-on-one isn't fair!" he shouted.

Kuzaku had a firm grip on Haruhiro's arms, Yume and Setora on his right leg, Shihoru and Merry his left leg.

"Ready, set...!"

On Kuzaku's orders, Haruhiro's body was first swung right, towards the shore. Picking up momentum like a pendulum, he then swung left towards the sea.

"Whoa, I'm not an object, so—"

"Go...!"

On Kuzaku's second signal, they all released him at once.

Uwah...

He was flying. Was he pulling some impressive air time here, maybe?

He was a bit scared, but it was pretty fun.

No, but when he started falling, the fear suddenly kicked in.

"Ahhhhhhhhhhhhhhhhhhhhhhhhhhhhhhhhh!!"

The reason he started flailing in mid-air was because he thought it would be more fun that way. Well, he had that much composure, at least.

Haruhiro landed in the water back first. But wasn't it deeper than he'd expected here? Not to the point his feet wouldn't touch the bottom, though. Instead of immediately floating back up, he took his time.

When he stuck his face out from the water, bellowing, "What was that foooooooor?!" in a loud voice, his comrades broke out laughing. Kuzaku was clutching his sides, tears in his eyes.

Haruhiro had been trying to get a laugh out of them, but was it really that funny? Normally Haruhiro wouldn't do things like this, so maybe the unexpectedness of it was making them happier about it. This wasn't so bad, once in a while. Only once in a while, though.

"Dammiiiiiit!" Haruhiro cut through the water, charging towards Kuzaku. The water was up to his shoulders and got deeper when the waves came, so even giving it his all, he didn't have much speed. He must have looked funny doing it, because everyone was laughing.

"Heyyyy!" Jimmy was shouting from the shore.

After watching, had he decided he wanted to join in? It didn't look like that was it, though.

With the coming waves, something passed by Haruhiro. Not just one thing. They came one after another, and some brushed Haruhiro as they went by. They were living creatures. Those sea-beast-like creatures that had been lying around on the beach, maybe?

"Ahhhh! Haruhiro!" Kuzaku's eyes were wide, and he was pointing at something.

"Haru! Behind you!" Merry's voice was raised.

Yume, Shihoru, and Setora were all shouting, too.

"Huh, behind—" Haruhiro turned around. "Wait, whaaaa-aaaaaaaaaaaa?!"

Something had opened its maw wide. Not one of those sea-beast-like creatures. It was a different creature. What could it be? Wait, now wasn't the time for wondering.

It was close. Super close. Was he going to get eaten?

Maybe—no, there was no maybe about it—he was in big trouble.

"Tahhh...!" Haruhiro let out a mysterious cry, and tried to jump to the left like his life depended on it, but he was caught in a powerful current, and he had no idea what happened.

But that meant he was still alive. He had apparently not been eaten.

The massive creature pressed through the water. More than the waves, the current created by that creature was throwing Haruhiro around. Was it a shark? A killer whale? Probably something along those lines.

Haruhiro shuddered. Normally, he'd have died there, wouldn't he? It still felt like he might die, too.

This was bad. He was going to drown.

Even when he managed to get his face up above the surface to take a breath, he swallowed a lot of water.

"Blech, salty!" he shouted.

Kuzaku and the others were screaming and running around wildly. Was that creature not a shark or a whale? It had gone up on land, and was attacking the sea-beast-like creatures one after another.

The tricks it was demonstrating, like using its well developed forearms to easily toss its prey, and jumping into the air on land to bite into them, were probably beyond what a shark or whale could do. The sea-beast-like creatures that had been lounging idly on the sandy beach now fled en masse back into the sea.

"It's no good," Haruhiro gasped. "When we get carried away, this stuff always happens!"

Haruhiro was heading for land, but the fleeing sea-beast-like creatures collided with him one after another, and he couldn't go where he wanted.

The shouting, roaring of animals, and screams all echoed.

The sun was setting.

Grimgar
of
Fantasy and Ash

10 | Cold Wind

NORTH OF RORONEA, it quickly turned into dense forest. That said, for the first thirty to forty meters, there was an area where the trees had been cut down, leaving a grassy plain. The grass had grown thick there before, but now it was thick with stalls and shops, all of which seemed to be open for business around the clock.

Haruhiro and the group bought a change of clothes at this emergency market north of Roronea. There wasn't a branch of the Yorozu Deposit Company, so they had little in the way of money. The selection of goods was also very "tropical," you might say. There were a lot of very showy outfits, and it was a little hard to choose, but the party managed somehow.

The dragons were angry. Someone had done something to anger them. No matter what anyone had done before, the dragons had never shown themselves outside of flying between their nest and fishing grounds.

If someone were going to do anything to the dragons, they would have to sneak into their nests. If they were going to approach the nests, they would have to pass through the dense forest.

The forest was home to the runarukas. The runarukas might know something.

With the runaruka pirate Tsiha leading the way, Haruhiro and the group entered the forest.

From what Tsiha told them, or rather Yume's feeling translation of it, the runarukas weren't especially secretive, but they were reserved. Even if the party called out to them, they wouldn't show themselves. However, if the group went to them and asked politely, there were probably some runarukas who would hear them out.

In addition, the runarukas generally woke up in the afternoon and were up all night. If the party wanted to meet them, it would actually be better to look by night.

Tsiha said it could lead the party to the village where its family lived.

Incidentally, Section Head Jimmy was elsewhere, investigating if there were any other rumors about the dragons.

Why were the dragons mad? Haruhiro had no clue, but they weren't rampaging around blindly. But if this was revenge, it was a little weak. Intimidation then, maybe? Maybe they were showing off their incomparable power, threatening the people of Roronea over something. Didn't it look like that?

In truth, one idea had popped into his head.

Eggs, or perhaps dragonets.

Had someone snuck into the dragons' nest and made off with their eggs or children?

He wasn't familiar with dragon ecology or their abilities, so this was only his imagination, but maybe they had followed their eggs' or children's scent, and discovered they were being hidden in Roronea. Then, because they couldn't speak to demand their children back, they were showing it through their actions.

He didn't know how large dragonets were, but given how large grown dragons were, they couldn't be small. They would probably cry or struggle, too, so eggs seemed the more likely possibility. Or perhaps the dragonets were already dead, and the parents believed they were still alive or something.

However, was there really enough value in them to justify the risk of stealing a dragon's egg or a dragonet?

He'd asked Jimmy, and gotten the response, *"I can't say there isn't."*

If they were the genuine artifact, there were any number of people who would want an egg or living dragonet, or even a dragonet's dead body.

Roronea was a town of pirates, but merchants came to trade with them, too. On those merchant or pirate ships, there were sometimes people of uncertain origins and objectives. Treasure hunters, you might call them. To give an example, explorers like Lala and Nono might do something like enter a forbidden zone like the dragons' nest, and carry off a dragon egg or dragonet. It wasn't impossible.

If something like that had, hypothetically, happened, it wouldn't be strange for a couple of people to have seen or heard something. That the dragons had only attacked the port once was interesting. This was, again, only his imagination, but at that time, the culprits might have been at the No. 2 Pier. That, or aboard one of the ships stopped there. So perhaps the culprit had made a narrow escape, and was now hiding in town. Thus, the dragons had been attacking Roronea ever since, trying to threaten the culprit into returning the egg or dragonet, or else.

There was no proof, so, as has been said repeatedly, this was all strictly Haruhiro's imagination. But someone had done something bad to the dragons. That someone was in Roronea. Or had been in Roronea, at least. Haruhiro was certain of that much.

If that person were clever, they might not have left any traces. Still, even if Haruhiro couldn't nab that person by the tail, there might be a single hair from that tail lying somewhere.

The forest was a scary place at night, but Haruhiro's party had experience with Darunggar and Thousand Valley, and they had Tsiha as a guide. They heard the cries of beasts or sensed their presence on a number of occasions, but nothing really happened as they walked for maybe two hours.

"Is it going to take much longer?" Kuzaku asked.

Yume asked Tsiha, "Time? Take? Long?"

She was just breaking it into single words, wasn't she?

"Lilmore," Tsiha answered.

Soon they saw what looked to be a fire up ahead. A torch or something like that, most likely. When they approached, it turned out to be a bonfire, and there was one runaruka standing next to it.

Tsiha greeted the other in the language of the runarukas, and the runaruka responded.

"Come," Tsiha said. "This way."

Tsiha pointed past the fire and led Haruhiro and the group on. The runaruka by the fire wore clothes like Tsiha, carried a bow and arrows over its shoulder, and had a hatchet at its waist. It didn't take its eyes off Haruhiro and the party until they had passed, but there was no particular hostility.

Still, it was strange. What was strange exactly? Haruhiro couldn't put it into words, but something bugged him.

"Tsiha," he called.

"Nngh?" Tsiha replied immediately.

"Do you come back to the runaruka village often?"

"No."

"Damn."

Haruhiro cursed despite himself, then moved fast. He drew his dagger, grappled Tsiha, and pressed it to the runaruka's throat.

"Haru-kun?!" Yume cried.

Kuzaku looked startled. "Whuh..."

"Be on guard!" Haruhiro shouted. "Don't move," he warned the struggling Tsiha. "You understand, right? What I'm saying. You've understood all along. You're trying to set us up, aren't you?"

Tsiha stopped resisting, but didn't respond.

Someone was approaching. The runaruka who had been by the fire before. It had an arrow nocked and drawn.

Setora tried to have Kiichi move quietly towards the darkness, and the runaruka loosed its arrow.

"Kih!" Kiichi cried and jumped back. He dodged the arrow by a hair's breadth, but it was a close call.

The runaruka was readying its next arrow. That runaruka was a pretty good shot.

"We screwed up," Setora muttered.

Indeed. They hadn't meant to, but they'd let their guards down.

"There's more..." was all Merry said.

Shihoru readied herself, letting out a relaxed breath.

To the front, right, and left, there were now sounds. They were deliberately choosing not to conceal their footsteps. *We're here, we're here,* they were telling the party.

When Kuzaku tried to draw his large katana, the runaruka with the bow ready shouted, "Ianna!" in a frightening voice.

"Sword, no draw," Tsiha said in a low voice. "Shoot arrow. Poison. Die fast."

"Kuzaku." Haruhiro shook his head.

Kuzaku removed his hand from the hilt of his large katana.

"Are you going to kill us?" Haruhiro asked.

"Tsiha not decide."

"Who decides?"

"Papa."

"Your father?"

"Tsiha's papa. Leader of Kamushika."

"Some sort of tribal leader?" Haruhiro mused. "Then you're the next in line to lead your tribe?"

"Have older brother."

It turned out the leader of the runarukas who had encircled the party and caught them in this trap was that older brother.

A runarauka that looked somewhat like Tsiha, but taller, and with a sturdier build, came forward, saying something in their language.

According to Tsiha's translation, if they kept quiet and didn't resist, they wouldn't be killed just yet. Furthermore, his brother was leading more than ten runarukas, and all of them were archers with their bows aimed at the party.

Haruhiro had no reason to doubt Tsiha's words about the arrows being coated with deadly poison. For now, it looked like they would have to do as they were told.

Their hands were bound tightly behind their backs with rope, and they were led off.

Kiichi initially bared his fangs at the approaching runarukas to intimidate them, but when Setora said, "Stop, Kiichi," he went quiet and was bound. The gray nyaa was carried by the runarukas like luggage.

Along the way, Setora mumbled things like, "They got us. I don't know how it turned out like this..."

Then she tripped over something and pushed Haruhiro lightly. "Ah!" she cried.

"Ianna!" one runaruka warned them.

"Sorry," Setora apologized meekly, moving away from Haruhiro.

In probably about half an hour, they came to a place where there were the lights of many bonfires, likely a village. How many of these elevated houses, built in the treetops, were there? It was kind of hard to tell. Even during the day, they'd be hidden by the trees, so it would be hard to work out. Still, this didn't look like it was a small village, by any means.

Many runarukas were waiting for Haruhiro and the party. Not just tens. Hundreds. There were two, three hundred of them. Looking at the size of them, it wasn't just adults. There were children mixed in, too. The clothes they wore likely came from Roronea. From the look of things, they had adjusted them to suit their bodies.

Every runaruka had a bow and arrows suited to its size slung over its shoulder. In addition, many of them carried hatchets, knives, or curved swords.

They all had fox faces, and it was pretty hard to determine their age just from size, but it seemed like the amount of hair they had increased with age. The small runarukas had little hair, while the ones that looked older were awfully furry.

Haruhiro and the party were made to sit in front of a large bonfire lit in the middle of the village.

Tsiha and the solidly built runaruka that was apparently Tsiha's brother were talking about something. The other runarukas were scrutinizing the group from a distance.

Very few runarukas went to Roronea, meaning the rest had little contact with the outside world, so maybe humans were an unusual sight to them.

"Do you think Tsiha was trickin' Yume and everyone all along?" Yume hung her head, clearly depressed.

"I don't think they were out to deceive us in particular." Even with her hands bound tight behind her, Setora was calm, sitting in a kneeling position, with her back straight. Kiichi, who was beside her, was imitating Setora's posture, which was kind of funny. "They may have infiltrated the K&K Pirate Company for some purpose, and pretending not to understand the human language must have been more convenient for them."

"Yume, she spent so much time talkin' with Tsiha, and she never even noticed..."

"Nah," Kuzaku said with a bitter laugh. "That's not just on you, Yume-san. None of us noticed, okay? I mean, even listening to you interpret, I never thought, 'Huh, that's suspicious,' or anything like that."

"Nuuuugh," Yume moaned. "Yume's a real dummy..."

Suddenly, making their way through the wall of runarukas, an especially fluffy runaruka appeared, accompanied by a big one.

When the two stopped in front of Haruhiro, the whole area went quiet.

The fluffy runaruka spoke. The big runaruka interpreted.

"Humans enter forest. Runarukas not allow. You are bad humans."

The big runaruka was slightly more fluent than Tsiha, which was a surprise.

Still, this runaruka was huge. He was taller than Kuzaku. He only wore a sleeveless vest on his upper half, but his chest had such girth that it looked like it was ready to burst. His neck, shoulders, and arms were thick, and his body was on another level from the other runarukas. He had the same fox face, but was he really a member of the same race?

"We're not bad humans," Haruhiro began, looking from the fluffy runaruka to the big runaruka. "Do you mind if I explain?"

Big translated the question, and Fluffy nodded.

"Speak," Big urged him.

Haruhiro took a breath. "I'm sure you runarukas are aware the dragons are attacking Roronea. We suspect that's because someone did something to anger them. We're looking for whoever it was. We want to figure out what it was they did. My thinking is that person must have entered the dragons' nest and stolen something."

Big whispered in Fluffy's ear, telling him Haruhiro's words.

Tsiha told them that if you say something frightening, the gewguw will come and make you sick. The runarukas likely believed that speaking about anything involving the dragons would bring in the gewguw. That was why Big was keeping his voice down so the other runarukas couldn't hear.

Fluffy was whispering something back to Big. Big nodded, then glared at Haruhiro.

"You are bad humans. Your words call cold wind."

One of the things about the gewguw was that, when it came, you could tell immediately because a cold wind would blow.

Maybe just talking about a taboo was enough to make Haruhiro a bad human in the eyes of the runarukas. Maybe, just maybe, was he going to get killed...?

No, the situation wasn't that dire. This wasn't a crisis he couldn't get out of.

Or so he thought. It was just instinct, really.

"We're not the bad humans," he told them. "They're elsewhere. Still hiding in Roronea. They did the bad thing. Is it okay to let them go?"

"That is your problem. Nothing to do with runarukas."

"We just want you to help a little."

"Runarukas will not get involved."

"At this rate, the pirates will abandon Roronea. If Roronea disappears, that'll be a problem for you people, too."

"Long ago, there was no Roronea," Big said. "Not a problem for runarukas."

Big was no longer bothering to interpret everything for Fluffy. If Fluffy was something like the tribal chief, Big might be his successor. That, or Big was the chief—in other words, Tsiha's papa—and Fluffy was the elder, or the former chief who'd moved into an advisor-like position.

Whatever the case, it was hard to tell how hard to press. If Haruhiro angered Big, it was possible he would be executed on the spot. It might be better not to be too aggressive, and to beg for his life instead.

"Papa." Tsiha stepped forward, saying something to Fluffy in the language of the runarukas.

It looked like Fluffy was Tsiha's father, after all.

"Tsiha!" Big scolded Tsiha.

Tsiha argued back with something, then kept talking to Fluffy.

It seemed Tsiha was arguing on their behalf. Haruhiro wondered what Tsiha was trying to do, after leading them into this trap and all, but if Tsiha was going to take their side, that helped.

Go for it, Tsiha.

If talks broke down, Haruhiro and his group might, at worst, have to resort to the use of force. If that happened, neither side would get off unharmed. There were children here, so he would prefer to avoid that.

Tsiha was still arguing passionately.

Haruhiro surveyed the surrounding area. If it came to it, what would he do?

The truth was, Haruhiro had a small, razor-like blade hidden, and he could cut his ropes at any time. Before reaching this village, Setora had deliberately bumped into him and passed it to him. She likely had one of her own, too. If Haruhiro and Setora felt like it, they could free themselves from their bonds immediately.

The runarukas had bound the party's hands, but they hadn't bothered to disarm them. It was hard to call them cautious.

The poison arrows warranted caution, but if the party quickly jumped into the crowd, the runarukas wouldn't be able to shoot them for fear of hitting the wrong target. There was the option of taking Chief Fluffy hostage, too. That might be the more practical solution.

If he was going to do it, it had to be by surprise, so he had to act before there was no other choice.

If Haruhiro moved, his comrades would surely react. He had no worry about that.

Tsiha was pointing at them and saying something in a violent tone.

Is it time?

Not yet?

If he screwed up, things would get really bad. That was true, but if he was overly conscious of failure, his body would tense up, and it would be difficult to exert his best efforts. He had to stop caring, to some degree. No matter what happened, he'd deal with it when it came up.

"Tuwanra, shitte!" Tsiha shouted, and the crown of runaruka onlookers roared, which worried Haruhiro a little.

"Tuwanra! Tuwanra! Tuwanra! Tuwanra!" The crowd stomped their feet and chanted that word.

They were really excited. Not good. In this situation, it was going to be hard to move.

Suddenly, the big runaruka thumped his thick chest. "Tuwanra! Clear the cold wind! I am Mwadan, first son of Papa Dutt, chief of the Kamushika! You humans, duel me, one-on-one!"

Haruhiro blinked twice. "...Huh? Duel? What?"

"Well, it's gotta be me, I guess." Kuzaku stood up.

The runarukas roared even louder.

"Tuwanra!"

"Tuwanra!"

"Tuwanra!"

"Tuwanra!"

"Tuwanra!"

"No, no, no." Haruhiro was half-dazed. "Why?" he mumbled.

"Huh?" Kuzaku turned back, looking down at Haruhiro. He had a mystified look on his face. "Can't I? The enemy's big, so I figured it'd be me."

"That's not really the problem here."

The runarukas were all fired up, and Mwadan the big runaruka was casting off his vest, clearly ready to go, and Kuzaku had a slight air of, *I'll take you! Bring it on!* around him, too. It looked they were going to be having a one-on-one duel.

Seriously, why?

11 | Give It Everything You've Got

THE LARGE FIRE was moved aside, and twelve smaller fires were built in a circle around the plaza.

No one but the chief of the Kamushika tribe, Papa Dutt, his eldest son Mwadan, and his opponent Kuzaku were allowed to enter the ring.

Haruhiro and the rest of the party were, of course, made to sit outside the ring.

Like Mwadan, Kuzaku was made to take off his armor, and was naked from the waist up.

Papa Dutt performed a body search on both parties, checking that neither had anything that could be used as a weapon. The duel would be carried out bare-handed.

Tsiha explained what was going on in clumsy human language. Tuwanra wasn't the duel itself, but a ritual held to drive away the gewguw. There was meaning in two fearless men risking their lives in a competition of strength, and the gewguw would run away in fear of their savage valor.

There were proper rules, too:

The use of weapons was prohibited.

If you left the ring, you lost.

If you died, you lost.

There was no surrender.

That was all.

It was refreshing how clear and simple that was. It seemed any attack was allowed so long as it didn't make use of a weapon, but according to Tsiha, fighting dirty wouldn't be looked upon kindly.

Fight fair, and kill each other with your bare hands, is that it? Isn't that pretty dangerous...?

In the middle of the ring, Papa Dutt wore a solemn expression. That is, he had a fox's face, so Haruhiro didn't really understand his expressions, but he got the feeling that was the kind of expression it was. Anyway, he was standing there with this solemn air about him.

Mwadan was at the edge of the ring, stretching, swinging his arms in circles, and diligently doing his warm-up exercises. The runarukas got worked up by every little thing that Mwadan did.

Looking around, there was no other runaruka built as impressively as him, so Mwadan might be something like a hero of the Kamushika people.

Incidentally, the Kamushika were only one tribe of runaruka, and they happened to be the largest on the main island.

Kuzaku was twisting his upper body, stretching his Achilles tendon, and focused on a variety of stretching exercises. Because he was moving his body in a slow, relaxed way, it seemed like he wasn't nervous at all, but who knew how he really felt.

"Kuzakkun!" Yume called out to him.

Kuzaku turned their way and grinned.

"He's awfully composed," Setora said, sitting upright, calm and self-composed herself.

Kiichi, who was beside her, had his ears perked up and seemed to have a bit more of a sense of urgency, but it might have just been that all the noise was keeping him from settling down.

"Kuzaku-kun, do your best!" Shihoru's voice was trembling. Her whole body was tense, and she was stiff.

This was Shihoru. The situation had to be harder on her than being in trouble herself.

Merry's face was tense, too. "If you get hurt, I'll heal you."

Kuzaku waved with both hands and flashed them a toothy grin. "'Kay! If that happens, I'm counting on you. Well, it'll be fine. I've got this."

Should Haruhiro say, *Those are some big words,* and tease him? Or he should simply encourage him?

Haruhiro was still deciding when Kuzaku gave him a silent thumbs-up.

There's no need for words between us, is that it?

Well, yeah.

Kuzaku's opponent seemed pretty confident in his abilities. This was hardly going to be a case where his size made him look tougher than he actually was. Kuzaku specialized in defending himself with his armor, helmet, and shield, fearlessly taking hits from the enemy, then aiming to strike back. If they were wrestling bare-handed, those tactics would be completely useless. That was why Haruhiro was worried, but Kuzaku was several meters away. He couldn't give him detailed advice. Still, he had the feeling that wasn't necessary, anyway.

When Haruhiro nodded, Kuzaku's face wrinkled up with a grin.

Why are you so happy? Haruhiro wondered. *Well, it's fine, I guess.*

"Ooozureee. Aaadiiistaaa. Deeeooobooo." Papa Dutt spread his arms wide, letting his sonorous voice echo.

"Tuwanra!"

"Tuwanra!"

The runarukas chanted, and Papa Dutt continued.

"Raaagareee. Soookiiiiiiyaaa. Rureeegaaaaaareee."

"Tuwanra!"

"Tuwanra!"

"Araaasute! Nanaaadiiiyaaa. Tuwanra!"

"Tuwanra!"

"Tuwanra!"

"Ooooseeeyooo, Kamushiakaooo, Mwadan!"

"Mwadan!"

"Mwadan!"

"Mwadan!"

"Waooooooooooooooooooooooooooooooo...!" Mwadan

howled, punching his fist towards the sky repeatedly as he moved forward.

"Oooseeeyooo, nuhaaagura, Kuzaaaku!"

When Papa Dutt called Kuzaku's name, all the runarukas bared their fangs, hissing as if booing him. Unwilling to let the crowd show them up, Haruhiro and the others repeated Kuzaku's name.

"Kuzakuuuuuuu!" Haruhiro shouted.

"Nyaaa! Kuzakkun! Kuzakkun!" cried Yume.

"Kuzaku-kun, hang in there!" called Shihoru.

"You show him, Kuzaku!" yelled Merry.

"Nyaaaooo!" That was Kiichi.

"Oh, yeahhhhhhhhhhh! Bring it onnnnnnnnnnnnn!" Kuzaku made gestures to provoke the runarukas as he approached Mwadan.

The two of them faced each other, with a gap of forty, fifty centimeters left between them.

Kuzaku was around one hundred and eighty centimeters tall, so that put Mwadan at about two meters. They were about equally wide, but Mwadan's body was far thicker. Especially his chest and waist, which seemed to jut out, and his arms and legs, which were wonderfully thick. Did his hair just make them look bigger? No, even factoring for that, Mwadan really did have way more muscle.

"Tuwanra, zei!" Papa Dutt gave the signal to start and backed away.

Neither Mwadan nor Kuzaku moved yet.

The runarukas called out "Mwadan, Mwadan," egging their hero on.

The two stared each other down, neither blinking.

First Mwadan moved his left leg back, and brought his hands up to the same level as his face. It looked like he was inviting Kuzaku to wrestle and compare their strengths.

In a simple test of muscular strength, the larger one had the advantage. But Kuzaku was calm. He didn't take Mwadan's invitation, swinging wide with his right fist instead.

The runarukas hissed in anger. They were probably criticizing Kuzaku as a coward for not accepting the test of strength.

Kuzaku, meanwhile, was going, *I'm gonna hit you! I'm gonna hit you real hard!* in an easy-to-understand manner, forcing a decision upon Mwadan.

"Ein!" Mwadan shouted in a way that felt like a, *Come at me!* digging in his heels and leaning forward. He prepared to stop Kuzaku's hand.

"Nnnnnnnnnnnguh!" Kuzaku swung at him. His hand was clenched tight, but it wasn't a punch. He didn't thrust his hand out; he more or less pushed it out while bringing it down sharply. The area from the base of his pinky finger to his wrist, that side of his hand, slammed into Mwadan's snout.

Mwadan reeled for a moment. Blood spurted from his nose. However, he didn't just hold his ground; he brought his hands together and raised them up.

"Dieeeeeeeeeeeeeeeeeeeee!" Mwadan's hands landed a direct blow on the back of Kuzaku's head.

For a moment, the sound made it seem like his head was torn off, but it hadn't been. Kuzaku ended up in a position unbelievably close to being on all-fours. Yet somehow he managed to stop himself and not fall over.

Mwadan snorted twice, clearing his left and right nostril of blood, then grappled Kuzaku. He leaned over the top of Kuzaku's back, grabbing him by the back of his thighs.

Did he mean to pick him up like that?

Yes, that was it exactly.

"Nwoahhh!" Mwadan lifted Kuzaku up, spinning him sideways. Kuzaku was lifted over Mwadan's head.

"Stop!" Shihoru practically screamed.

The runarukas chanted, "Mwadan! Mwadan! Mwadan! Mwadan!" urging their hero on.

Haruhiro ground his teeth. He didn't shut his eyes.

Mwadan slammed Kuzaku into the ground. No, that would have been better than what he actually did. It was different. He didn't do that.

Mwadan knelt. He brought Kuzaku down not on the ground, but on his right knee.

You'll break it. If you do that. You'll break his back.

Kuzaku rolled from Mwadan's right knee onto the ground.

Mwadan stood up, raising his right fist.

"Ohhhhhhhhhhhhhhhhhhhhhhhhhhhhhhhhhhhhhh!" the crowd cried.

"Mwadan!"

"Mwadan!"

"Mwadan!"

"Mwadan!"

The runarukas roared.

Kuzaku was face down, immobile. He was pressing his left arm against his back.

Can't he move? No way, did his back actually break?

"Kuzaku...!" Haruhiro started to stand despite himself, but someone pressed down on his shoulders from behind and stopped him. It was Tsiha.

"No stand."

Mwadan slowly circled the ring as he walked over to Kuzaku. Surrender would not be accepted. Would Mwadan try to force Kuzaku out of the ring? Or would he finish him?

The runarukas probably wanted a final conclusion. It was hard to see Mwadan betraying that expectation. He'd probably meant to end this by killing Kuzaku in the ring from the beginning.

Yume and Shihoru were cheering hard, but Merry and Setora were very quiet.

Haruhiro forced himself to breathe.

As party leader, Haruhiro had watched Kuzaku all this time. As a comrade, too. And also, probably, as a friend. That's why he understood. Kuzaku hadn't lost the will to fight yet.

Isn't that right, Kuzaku?

Mwadan tried to kick Kuzaku.

He stopped.

"Hadda! Hadda!" The runarukas urged him to hurry. *Do it! Kill him!* they were no doubt saying.

Mwadan went to kick him, then stopped. There was a little booing from the crowd.

It might look otherwise, but Mwadan was apparently quite cautious. He'd probably been testing Kuzaku's response. However, even after he'd tried to attack him twice, Kuzaku hadn't budged. That last attack must have hit him pretty hard.

What a pushover. I'll at least end this with a big move to satisfy the crowd. That may have been what Mwadan thought.

In order to pick Kuzaku up again, he crouched down and reached out with both arms. That was when it happened.

Kuzaku sprang up, head-butting Mwadan in the chin.

Mwadan's head flew back, and Kuzaku went on a fierce offensive.

His fists. With his left and right fist, he pummeled Mwadan's face.

After taking a number of good punches, Mwadan covered his face with his arms. Kuzaku didn't care, and showered him with punches from above his guard. He meant to forcefully break down his guard.

"Suh!" Maybe sensing the danger, Mwadan tried to hit Kuzaku in the left flank with a roundhouse kick using his right foot.

Kuzaku must have seen it coming. He didn't avoid it, instead grabbing Mwadan's right leg with his left arm. "Hahhhhhh!"

He pushed Mwadan down, mounted him, and hammered away at him. Mwadan's face was getting pummeled.

The runarukas screamed.

Mwadan was trying to do something to defend himself from Kuzaku's assault, but it wasn't working. Mwadan was already bloodied. He was less and less able to defend himself.

Finally, Mwadan ended up spread-eagled. Had he gone down, maybe?

Kuzaku could win. The odds were overwhelmingly good that this was a win. Now he just had to finish it. The question was how.

Kuzaku jumped away from Mwadan.

A ring out. If he could force him out of the ring without taking his life, nothing could be better.

That thought crossed Haruhiro's mind, and probably Kuzaku's, too. It wasn't naive thinking.

Kuzaku tried to grab Mwadan's right ankle. Mwadan probably wasn't imitating Kuzaku from earlier, but in that instant, he seemed to wake up and went on a counterattack. Still lying on the ground, he kicked. He kicked Kuzaku with both his feet.

When Kuzaku backed away, Mwadan immediately got up.

Springing at him, Mwadan swung out with his hands and feet. He wasn't using well-polished techniques, by any means, but he had intensity. If he were against Haruhiro, even one of those hits would have knocked his soul from his body.

Kuzaku wasn't forced entirely on the defensive; he attacked, too. Or rather, he got hit, and he hit back. Hit back and was hit again. When he hit, he was hit, and when hit, he hit.

Neither was blocking.

Mwadan had been bloody to begin with, but at some point

Kuzaku also ended up bruised all over his face, chest, and sides. He was bleeding all over.

"Mwadan!"

"Mwadan!"

"Mwadan!"

"Mwadan!"

The runarukas called the name of their hero.

"Kuzaku!"

"Kuzakkun!"

"Kuzaku-kun!"

"Kuzaku!"

"Kuzakuuuu!"

"Nyaaaooooon!"

All Haruhiro and the party could do was believe in Kuzaku's victory, and cheer until their voices were hoarse.

Mwadan made a big swing with his right arm and clobbered Kuzaku. Intentionally or not, Kuzaku ducked his head a bit. Thanks to that, Mwadan's right fist caught him square in the side of the head. That seemed to hurt Mwadan's right hand, but he still used it to slap Kuzaku.

Kuzaku either didn't or couldn't dodge, because he kept getting slapped by Mwadan.

Suddenly, Mwadan stopped moving. He was apparently out of breath. In that instant, Kuzaku closed the gap between them. He wrapped his arms around Mwadan's neck, pulled him towards him, and slammed his knee into Mwadan's flank.

Again and again.

"Ahhh! Ahhhh! Nwahhhhh!" Kuzaku shouted.

Mwadan didn't try to throw Kuzaku off, instead choosing to accept the blows.

"Nngh! Nnnnngh! Gunnnnnnngh!"

Eventually, the two stumbled apart.

Next was Mwadan's turn. Everyone knew that.

Of course, Mwadan ran forward, then jumped. It was a jumping kick with both his feet together. No matter how beaten up Kuzaku was, he should have been able to dodge that.

But Kuzaku didn't dodge. He tried to deflect Mwadan's feet with his chest. That was crazy. Kuzaku was flipped over, but Mwadan fell to the ground.

Neither got up immediately.

The runarukas chanted Mwadan's name, while the party chanted Kuzaku's.

Mwadan got up, and so did Kuzaku.

There was a storm of applause.

"Udaaa! Come!" Mwadan beckoned. Kuzaku backed away a number of steps, giving himself a run up.

"Dwahrahhhhhhhhhh!"

It was no ordinary jump kick. Kuzaku let loose with a jumping roundhouse kick into the side of Mwadan's face.

Mwadan was mowed down, and while Kuzaku was thrown off balance, he somehow managed to catch himself just short of falling.

This was a first. Kuzaku received roaring applause from the runarukas.

"Yeahhhhhhhhhhhhhhhhhh!" Kuzaku thrust his fist into the air in response, then turned towards the fallen Mwadan. "Get up! Come on, up! I know you can still fight! This isn't all you've got! No way!"

Mwadan first rolled to the side, lying face down, then used all his arms and legs to push himself up.

"Mwadan!"

"Mwadan!"

"Mwadan!"

"Mwadan!"

"Mwadan!"

Kuzaku and Mwadan were both amazing. Truly incredible. Haruhiro needed Kuzaku to win, obviously. But still, he didn't want to see Mwadan suffer a miserable defeat, either.

The fever in the air was probably dulling his decision-making capabilities. Haruhiro felt like such a downer for thinking this way. Yes, they were incredible and all. Sure. But where was the need for them to both keep taking hits like that? They ought to defend or dodge more. Were they stupid?

More than happy to be idiots, Kuzaku and Mwadan both puffed up their chests, not belittling their opponent, and trying to show off their own strength.

How's that? I'm tough, right?

I'm tougher.

Then I'm even tougher than you.

I'll do you one better.

Kuzaku and Mwadan stumbled towards one another.

When Mwadan thrust out his left fist, Kuzaku caught it lightly with his left hand. Mwadan's right hand was hurt, and he couldn't make a fist with it anymore.

The two of them both took a step back.

Kuzaku stepped forward first, punching Mwadan.

Mwadan hit Kuzaku back.

Next it was Kuzaku.

Then Mwadan.

They clobbered each other.

They had both been beaten black and blue, and were thoroughly exhausted, but they put their entire soul into each hit. They had to hurt.

Would it be Mwadan? Or Kuzaku? Which would kneel first?

With both the feeling of *I don't care who wins, just end it quickly,* and *Don't lose, Kuzaku,* both caught in his throat, Haruhiro could hardly breathe. It was mind-numbing.

It'll probably end with the next blow.

But then it didn't.

Well, maybe this time.

Not yet?

This next one has to be it.

Still not yet?

The punches kept flying back and forth for a long time, and he started to wonder if it ever would end.

Mwadan's right fist slammed into Kuzaku's cheek. The right fist he shouldn't have been able to make anymore. The runarukas cheered, and Haruhiro very nearly called his name, too.

Kuzaku stumbled. There was a smile on his messed-up face. "Hwahahh."

What had he been trying to say? Kuzaku could no longer speak properly. Even so, he didn't fall.

It was Mwadan who collapsed.

Mwadan fell to both knees as if his waist had given out. Then, as Mwadan was about to fall forward, Kuzaku caught him.

Mwadan was clearly unconscious. It was plain to see that his whole body had gone limp. Even so, Kuzaku took Mwadan's right arm and raised it up high.

Setora shook her head slightly.

Shihoru and Yume were staring at Kuzaku.

Merry nodded.

The runarukas' cry pierced the heavens.

Haruhiro finally let out a sigh.

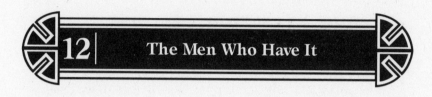

12 | The Men Who Have It

THINKING ABOUT IT CALMLY, there was no real winner, and ending things acting like both of them were winners seemed kind of off, but the tuwanra was just a ritual to drive the gewguw away.

The only thing that was important was whether the runarukas thought, *Okay, the gewguw won't come now, we're fine,* or not.

In that sense, everyone had a great time. In practical terms, Mwadan had lost, but that was only because the human he'd faced was incredibly strong.

And that strong man had praised their hero.

It had been a close fight. Either could have won. Therefore, it was not only the human who had won, but Mwadan as well, or so the runarukas felt the human champion had shown them.

For Kuzaku's part, he just felt a sense of accomplishment and release, going with what he felt like at the moment, but if the runarukas could accept it more that way, that made it the best choice anyway.

Thus, the tuwanra was accomplished.

Kuzaku and Mwadan had their wounds healed immediately by Merry's Sacrament.

When Mwadan awoke from being unconscious, the runarukas brought alcohol and started throwing a party.

The runarukas' alcohol came from fermenting the sap of the rati tree, producing a thick, white liquid with a sweet and sour taste and a good mouthfeel. Maybe it had low alcoholic content, because the runarukas drank it like water. Even the runaruka children were using stalks of grass like straws to slurp it up.

One had to wonder if it might not be better for them to wait until they were adults, but no one stopped them. It didn't seem there was a drinking age.

Kuzaku and Mwadan were both bare-chested, arms around each other's shoulders, competing to see who could drink more.

The runarukas now respected Kuzaku just as much as Mwadan and wanted to get closer to him. It was like they were racing to see who could pour his next drink the fastest. Seeing that, Mwadan let out a laugh of sincere joy, slapping Kuzaku on the back repeatedly. It looked like the hero of the Kamushika tribe was a magnanimous sort.

Yume, Shihoru, Merry, and Setora were caught by the runaruka women. Well, that said, the runarukas decided whether to become male or female when they reached adulthood, and Haruhiro wasn't sure how to tell one sex from the other by appearance. Still, somehow the runarukas around Yume and the girls all seemed female.

But, wait, could the runarukas really choose what sex they became? It was a mystery.

Haruhiro relied on Tsiha's interpretation skills to speak with Papa Dutt. Papa Dutt repeatedly pushed alcohol on Haruhiro, and it looked like he'd get upset if he refused, so Haruhiro did his best to drink as he asked about this and that.

Now that the gewguw was driven off, it apparently wouldn't return to this area for some time, so Papa Dutt wasn't even afraid to tell him about the frightening things anymore.

It seemed it wasn't just the Kamushika tribe who felt that way; the dragons were like gods to all of the runaruka.

That didn't mean there were no foolish runarukas who attempted to see those gods, though. Not many runarukas were foolish enough to enter the dragons' nest, but there were indeed some. These insolent runarukas were, on most occasions, killed by the dragons and never returned. However, there were also runarukas who did return.

One runaruka known as Yadikya of the Tatsuami tribe had brought a dragonet back to his village in an attempt to raise it. His goal must have been to raise the dragon, giving him power equal to a god. But instead he incurred the gods' wrath, and was given a clear show of their power.

The dragons had attacked the village of the Tatsuami tribe to take back the dragonet. Yadikya had been killed first, then eaten.

The Tatsuami had quivered in fear and released the dragonet, but the dragon gods would not forgive them. The village was destroyed, and the Tatsuami vanished from the face of this world.

Before that, "Yadikya" had been a common name, but it was now seen as a cursed name that might bring the gewguw. Now, except for after a tuwanra, it was forbidden to say that name.

The Yadikya incident had been a major trauma for the runarukas. Listening to Papa Dutt, it seemed the reason runarukas maintained strict taboos against getting close to the dragons or walking towards their nest was because of Yadikya's stunt.

To take it a step further, the Yadikya incident may have been what led to them worshiping the dragons as gods.

On very rare occasions, the runarukas would find a dragon scale in the forest. Those gleaming green dragon scales, especially if they were unscratched, were highly valuable, and the runarukas who found them were greatly blessed. However, they were not allowed to keep them.

The runarukas didn't have much of a concept of personal property to begin with, and they lived sharing most things among themselves, but the dragon scales didn't become communal property; the runarukas performed a ritual called sinatta and returned them to the sea. By doing that, the dragon gods would be pleased, and everyone in the tribe would be made happy.

In fact, runarukas who lived in Roronea like Tsiha had a job they were given. In exchange for being allowed to live outside the village, they had to keep watch on the pirates. If the pirates picked up a dragon scale, runarukas like Tsiha were to steal it somehow, and bring it back to the forest. If anyone tried to enter the forest excessively, or a runaruka heard someone was planning to harm the dragons, they had to notify the village.

Tsiha had become a pirate because of its longing for the world outside. However, it was a proud runaruka, and it loved its people. So it tried to carry out that duty.

After explaining that, Tsiha defended itself, saying it had never thought Haruhiro and his comrades were bad people, but just investigating the dragons was enough to upset the runarukas. If Tsiha had treated those humans as guests and invited them to the village, Papa Dutt and the other runarukas would surely have been angry. That was why, though it involved tricking the party, Tsiha had them captured temporarily. Tsiha had then intended to negotiate with Papa Dutt and get his cooperation somehow.

Was that really true? It felt pretty suspicious, but Tsiha was the one who had persuaded the runarukas to hold the tuwanra, and Kuzaku's performance had turned the Kamushika tribe friendly. That was a fact, so, well, though there were things Tsiha could stand to reflect on, all was well that ended well.

"So, we want to know why the dragons are angry," Haruhiro said. "I think someone—not one of you runarukas, but a pirate, or a resident of Roronea, or someone else from outside—definitely did something to anger the dragons. Do you have any ideas?"

When Tsiha translated Haruhiro's question, Papa Dutt stroked his fluffy chin and nodded.

"Papa, yes, saying," said Tsiha, interpreting for Papa Dutt. "Humans, dragon nest, try to enter. Three people. One, other runaruka, not Kamushika, killed. Two people, run."

"What happened to them after they ran?"

"Do not know," said Tsiha. "Tsiha did not know. About this. Not come back to village. Heard now. Papa—"

When Tsiha asked something, Papa Dutt explained, including hand gestures as he did.

"One month before, about. Two ran. After that, runarukas see no one. Probably them, pirates."

"Three pirates went through the forest and tried to enter the dragons' nest, but the runarukas found them," Haruhiro pondered. "They lost one of their comrades, so do you think they gave up?"

"Not go through forest," said Tsiha. "Not whole way. Just a little going through forest. Dragon nest, going with road. Is one."

"Another route? Going by pirate ship, maybe?" Haruhiro asked.

"Yes. Runaruka, not often, go out sea."

"But this is an island. I'd have thought you'd go fishing."

"Yadikya. Tatsuami. Many fish caught. Tatsuami die. After that, number of runarukas catch fish drop."

"Oh, so that's it... The dragon's wrath even changed your lifestyle."

"Kamushika, change, not like."

"You mean that, whatever anyone may have done, you don't want to get caught in the crossfire, right?"

"But dragon make angry. Not good."

"You want the dragons' rage to subside."

"Yes."

"We'll make sure there's no trouble for the runarukas. We have no intention of making you do anything that would upset them. I'd like you to be assured of that."

"Kamushika, you people trust. Tsiha. Tsiha's brother Mwadan. Tsiha's brother Tanba. Help you."

Tanba had to be that well-built runaruka that looked a little like Tsiha.

"Thanks," Haruhiro said gratefully. "That really helps."

"Dragons' nest, pirates approached. Ishakk, runaruka, killed one."

"Runarukas from the Ishakk tribe killed one of the pirates?"

"Yes. Two pirates ran. Tanba look into. Tanba, Ishakk, get along."

"Tanba will ask the Ishakk about things for us, you mean? But why do you think those pirates tried to go to the dragons' nest? No, they probably failed the first time, then tried again, taking a route along the coast... Would there happen to be a lot of dragon scales at the dragons' nest?"

"Dragons' nest, do not know. Runaruka do not go."

"That figures. But I feel they should be in the nest. They get scraped off, I'll bet. I'm sure a dragon's scales would sell for a high price. No, but would just gathering scales be enough to anger the dragons...?"

The Kamushika tribe's party went on until the sky began to brighten. The party was all made to drink a lot, until one and then another keeled over, and when they woke, it was close to noon.

Maybe it was an effect of the rati tree, but no one was badly hung over, so they returned to Roronea with Tsiha's guidance.

When they left, a large group of runarukas saw them off. Mwadan hugged Kuzaku repeatedly, to the point that some of the party members tilted their heads to the side and wondered if the two of them hadn't gotten closer in a kind of different way.

When they reached Roronea, the sun was beginning to set again, and three dragons were flying in the sky. Haruhiro and the party met up with Jimmy at the emergency marketplace.

"Find anything?" Jimmy asked.

"A bit," said Haruhiro. "How about on your end, Section Chief?"

"There was something I heard that caught my attention. There's this man called Benjamin, and—"

Roronea had once been controlled by the Skull Pirate Gang under Dead Skull, with terrible oppression. Later, the volunteer soldier trainee Kisaragi had defeated Dead, and peace had returned to the lives of the Emerald Archipelago's pirates.

The Skull Pirates had been dismantled, with more than half of Dead's underlings departing from Roronea. However, some had remained there.

There was no shortage of pirates who hadn't been a part of the Skull Pirate Gang by choice, but who had followed Dead's orders out of fear for their lives. Kisaragi didn't expel people just for having once been Dead's underlings.

In the world of pirates, heads of groups changing and groups coming together or breaking apart wasn't unusual in the least. There were any number of pirates who kept traveling from one gang to the next. In fact, some said that pirates who had only been in a single gang were in the minority.

So, Benjamin Fry was a Skull Pirate Gang remnant who had joined the Torokko Pirate Gang, soon quit, then changed his allegiance to the Dia Pirate Gang.

The Torokko and Dia pirate gangs were both small groups with only one medium-sized ship. Both of those gangs were now under the umbrella of the K&K Pirate Company.

To Section Chief Jimmy, Benjamin was a low rank employee of a subcontracting company, but this Benjamin guy had been quite close to Dead Skull once upon a time. He might not have been the man's right or left hand, but he had been one of the man's close confidantes.

At some point, after screwing up or doing something else to displease Dead, he had been demoted and become a common pirate. From that point on, he had never really stood out, so when the Skull Pirate Gang was brought to ruin, he had easily moved on to a new gang.

He still held a grudge against the old man, so he often said stuff like, *How pathetic,* and, *Glad he's gone,* apparently.

His nickname was Red-Eyed Ben.

Of all things, when he was younger, he'd taken a wound to his left eye that was left untreated, so the whites of his eye were now yellow, his pupil a reddish brown.

Pirates often tried to stand out with injuries, bizarre tattoos, or accessories. Benjamin was like that, too.

His age was uncertain, but he looked to be in his forties. He was bearded, and his chin was somewhat upturned. He had a straight figure, with short legs and oddly long arms.

Red-Eyed Ben, or Benjamin Fry, had up and vanished over a month ago, without a word to the captain of the Dia Pirate Gang. Not just Ben, either. Another young pirate called Step, and another called Honey Den, had left at the same time as Ben.

Step was a lanky man of around twenty, and liked gambling but lost a lot. Honey Den, who had a weakness for sweets, had come from the Skull Pirate Gang like Ben. He was a lazy man and blamed it on the pain of his cavities, and no one had so much as a single good thing to say about him.

Hearing all this, Haruhiro murmured, "One month ago, three pirates..."

It matched what they had heard from Papa Dutt.

Jimmy continued. "I hear Benjamin suddenly came back to Roronea thirteen days ago. Honey Den was with him."

"And Step?"

"It was just the two of them."

Out of the group of three pirates who had tried to enter the dragons' nest, one had been killed by the Ishakk tribe. This matched, too.

The captain of the Dia Pirate Gang had demanded answers from Ben and Honey Den, but they had kept mum about the reason for their disappearance, refusing to talk about anything to do with it. They both claimed neither knew what had happened to Step.

The captain, of course, had informed them they were fired, and told the other captains not to let the two of them on their ships.

In the world of pirates, it was apparently common to do this to a crew member who acted dishonorably towards you. It wasn't guaranteed it would be enforced, but neither Ben nor Honey Den were the likable sort to begin with. That, and they were former Skull Pirate Gang members, too. The pirate gangs of the Emerald Archipelago would likely have nothing to do with them.

However, they now seemed unconcerned by this, drinking, buying women, and gambling. It wasn't that they were partying so hard as to draw attention, but Ben happened to win big once while gambling.

Recently, he had said something like, "Yeah, men who've got it are different," and the pirates in the gambling den with him had thought it was a little strange.

"Men who've got it." What did he have? Generally, well, he'd probably mean luck.

He only won by chance. What's this old man running his mouth for? the other pirates had probably thought. *The pirates of the Emerald Archipelago won't bother with him anymore, but here he is, getting in a tizzy over one lucky win? Man, he's hopeless. I hope I never fall this far...*

It wasn't clear what had happened to him since the dragons began flying over Roronea, but when the first attack came, the two of them had been riding on the Ukobaku Pirate Gang's ship the *Great Tiger-go*.

The Ukobaku Pirate Gang possessed three pirate ships, and were not under the umbrella of the K&K Pirate Company. However, those two hadn't been aboard as crew, but as passengers. They'd made an agreement that they would be let off in the Coral Archipelago, and paid the captain of the *Great Tiger-go* a fair chunk of money for that.

On that day, two ships had been moored at the No. 2 Pier. One of them was the *Great Tiger-go*.

The *Great Tiger-go* was now destroyed beyond all recognition, and her remains still hadn't been removed.

The captain and five of her crew had shared the fate of their ship. Red-Eyed Ben had apparently gotten away. Honey Den was hurt badly, but he was holding on to his life, and like the other wounded, he had been treated by a gray elf shaman. But then he'd taken off without paying for the treatment.

"Wow, they sound like total scum..." Kuzaku said, a look of disgust on his face.

"So, where are Red-Eyed Ben and Honey Den now?" Haruhiro asked.

Jimmy gestured as if to say, *Follow me.*

The emergency market in the north was bustling, and they had to push past the people eating at chairs in front of pop-up stalls and other people walking by in order to get where they were going.

Looking up, the sight of the dragons flying over Roronea caught their eyes, and it was quite the surreal situation.

Jimmy suddenly came to a stop, indicating something ahead of them with his chin. There was a stall there, and pirates drinking. No chairs. The pirates were all standing drinking, or sitting on the ground as they tilted back their drinks.

Leaning against one of the stall's poles, a pirate who held his cheek with one hand as he drank caught their eye.

"That person, he has bad cavities," Merry whispered.

It was true; when his teeth peeked out as the pirate curled his lips back to take a sip from his mug, every one of them was brown. They weren't just discolored because they were dirty; they had gotten smaller, as if eaten away by germs.

Shihoru frowned, while Yume went, "Funyo?" and cocked her head to the side.

"Oh..." Kuzaku looked to Haruhiro.

Setora held Kiichi, stroking his throat.

Haruhiro nodded. "Honey Den, huh?"

Grimgar
of
Fantasy and Ash

13 | An Ugly Trick

"HONEY DEN," Haruhiro called out. "May we have a word?"

As he approached, Honey Den didn't say, *Yeah,* or, *What?* He just suddenly threw his mug at Haruhiro.

He might have been lazy, but contrary to appearances, he wasn't slow. Haruhiro managed to dodge the wooden mug itself, but he got a little bit of the booze on him.

Clicking his tongue, he chased after the fleeing Honey Den.

Without so much as a *Hey,* or an *Out of the way,* Honey Den pushed down people as he went and ran over them. It was the right way to flee in a crowd, but hard for any decent person to do. He apparently had no concern for his fellow man.

"You're scum!" Haruhiro shouted.

As he jumped over one of the fallen people, Haruhiro let out that insult despite himself, but Honey Den turned his head back and shouted, "Shut up! I'll kill you, you piece of crap!"

"You're the piece of crap!" Setora snapped.

For Honey Den, it must have felt as if, suddenly, a single woman had risen up to stand in his way.

The fact was, they had planned for the possibility he would bolt, and the party was spread out across the area. Honey Den had happened to pick the direction Setora was in.

Setora tried to sweep Honey Den's leg. Or rather, she gave Honey Den's shin the hardest kick she could muster.

"Gweh?!" Honey Den pitched forward and fell. He tried to get right back up, but Setora was on him in no time, putting her foot on his back.

"You think I'd let you escape, you moron?" she snarled.

"Nughhhhhhh..."

As Honey Den groaned, Kiichi ran over to him, hissing and baring his fangs threateningly.

"Whuh?! The hell?! A cat?! S-stop! Don't bite! I don't taste any good..."

"As if I'd let him eat you," Setora said contemptuously.

When Setora put her whole weight on her heel, Honey Den let out a kind of creepy squeal. Was he kind of enjoying this? He was seriously creepy...

Either way, Honey Den was now successfully captured. They would have loved to make him talk and be done with him here, but a bunch of curious gawkers had gathered around, so there was no time for that.

The sun was setting, and the dragons had flown off, so Haruhiro and the party escorted Honey Den into Roronea. That still attracted a lot of onlookers who, despite knowing nothing,

loudly shouted that they wanted to hit him, tear him apart, and kill him.

What to do?

Jimmy offered a suggestion.

"How about using our ship? It should be coming into port about now."

When they headed to the port, the *Mantis-go* was coming alongside the pier. For some reason, the K&K's KMW Momohina was on the gunwale, not the deck, doing what looked like kung-fu practice. Maybe that was part of her charm...or not? It was hard to tell.

Nothing could be said on that point, but the gunwale was no wider than a simple handrail, and just standing on it at all was terrifying. Despite that, she was doing flips, and screaming high kicks.

Seriously? It was inhuman.

"Mew, that's so cool..." Yume let out a sigh of admiration, and it wasn't hard to understand why, but Haruhiro would really rather she not start aspiring to be like that.

Once they helped with the mooring and boarded the *Mantis-go,* that noisy sahuagin Ginzy met with Haruhiro and the party, acting like he was the captain.

He was too noisy to bear. Best to ignore him.

"Hey, hey, hey! I'm the captain of this ship, I'll have you know!! What are you ignoring me for?! Hey, what for?! Damn it, I'll sue! No, I'd love to sue, but where can I?! Who will hear my pleas?! Hey, hey, hey, hey?! Hey! I said, hey!"

"Whewwww. Shut your mouth, dummy!" Momohina attacked Ginzy as she came down from the gunwale, easily lifting him up and giving him a hearty toss.

"Eeeeeeeeeeeeeeeeeeeeeeeeeeeeeeeeeeeeeeek!" His arms and legs flailing pathetically, Ginzy fell straight into the sea.

Sploosh! There was a great splash, and then he just sunk.

He floated back up a little later, making a fuss again. "What was that for, out of nowhere?! I know I'm a sahuagin, but this is too much! I'm not a sea sahuagin, I'm a land sahuagin, so the sea water's too salty. I'm halfway to being a freshwater fish, even though I'm not a fish, okay?! I'm stiiiiiiiiiiiiiiiiiiiiiiill the captain, though!"

They ignored him, and got on with the interrogation in the ship's hold. She must not have had anything to do, because Momohina tagged along.

Once the crew cleared out, the party and Momohina bound Honey Den to a pillar in the hold, and started the interrogation by asking if he'd gone into the forest with Red-Eyed Ben and Step.

"I have no idea what you're on about," the man whined. "Oww, it hurts. My teeth hurt."

Kuzaku cracked his knuckles, taking a threatening attitude. "This guy doesn't seem to get the situation he's in, does he?"

Honey Den just sneered a little.

Shihoru threw a *What now?* glance in Haruhiro's direction. It was hard to decide.

The pirates were ruffians, so they might use physical pain to extract a confession, but Haruhiro would honestly prefer not to be so uncivilized. Kuzaku was only making the threat. Basically, they were just posturing.

Merry said calmly, "If you need to make him hurt a bit, so long as he's still breathing, I can back you up."

At those unsettling words, Honey Den's expression changed just a little. "Heh. No matter what you do to me, I don't know what I don't know. I can't tell you anything I have no clue about. Oww, my teeth hurt."

"Hey, hey, Haru-kun," Yume started to say. "This person, he says his teeth hurt, so why not try takin' them out for him?"

"You say some scary things, Yume..."

"Isn't that a bit weak?" Setora sniffed.

She was blatantly looking down on Honey Den. He might have been the type she hated. Well, Haruhiro kind of hated him, too. Really hated him, maybe.

"He can only act tough for now," she said contemptuously. "Cut off a finger or two. If you do that, he'll tell you anything, I guarantee it."

"Don't underestimate me, you tramp!" Honey Den screamed.

"If you want to live to see the dawn tomorrow, keep your slobber in your mouth, pirate."

"I...I ain't scared of nothing! I mean it!"

"Do you want to see if you can still say that once I pluck out your eyeball and shove your severed ear into the socket?"

"Wh-what's with her?! I-Is she nuts?! No sane person comes up with things like that, right?!"

"I have reason to be used to cutting up dead bodies," Setora said coolly. "If they are still alive, that is of little consequence. Perhaps I should use you to prove that right now."

"I-I-I-I-If you think you c-can do it, b-bring it on! I-I-I-I can't t-tell you what I d-d-d-don't know!"

"Where should I start?" Setora pulled out a small blade and took a step toward Honey Den. She was perfectly expressionless, without a hint of hesitation in her voice or actions. "Why don't I skin that hideous face of yours? They often say fresh air tastes good, and without your skin, maybe you'll be able to taste it with your face. Want to try?"

"Y-y-y-y-you can't do that! I won't taste anything! It'll just hurt! It'll hurt like hell just getting my face skinned, too!"

"It may hurt so badly that you want to bite your tongue and die, but that does not concern me in the least."

"D-don't you have any human conscience?! There's something wrong with you!"

"Think what you will; it has no influence on me." Setora took another step towards Honey Den.

She couldn't possibly mean to go through with it...or so Haruhiro hoped, but Setora might very well do it without batting an eye. That was how she made them feel.

Was that part of the act? Probably. Hopefully it was just an act.

Now, as for whether he felt sorry for Honey Den...no, not in the slightest, but Haruhiro didn't want to think he had no choice but to let Setora get her hands dirty. He moved to stop Setora.

"Hold on, Sis!" Momohina cried.

He was beaten to it.

Momohina stepped up, still sweaty from kung-fu practice, so she just had her coat over her shoulders, not done up. She hadn't been wearing it before, but at some point she'd put the fake mustache back on.

"Who are you calling Sis?" Setora asked, looking disappointed.

"Heh..." Momohina laughed. "You're a sis, so I called you Sis, Sis."

"I don't understand..."

"Have no feeeear. I don't understand it myself, either!"

"KMW, was it?" Setora asked coolly. "Will you torture this rotten, cavity riddled piece of trash instead of me?"

"Pirates have pirate-yyyyyyyyyy wayssssssss of doing thangs."

"...Thangs?"

"Thoings? Hm? Did I get it wrong?"

"I don't think either is correct..."

"Whuddever. Pirates have their own way of doing things. That's right! Full speed ahead! On that note, Jimmy-chan, the thing, get the thing ready!"

Momohina seemed to be referring to some specific thing, but no matter how you looked at him, Jimmy seemed confused.

"What is the thing?" he asked.

"Fungh?!" Momohina's eyes went wide, and she beckoned Jimmy over to whisper in his ear.

Jimmy nodded, left the hold, and came back shortly with it in his arms.

"Yes! Thiiiis is what a pirate should use!" Momohina lifted the bundle of large bird feathers she had received from Jimmy up high.

Jimmy had brought a pot, too. Momohina dipped the feather in that pot.

"I-Is that...?" Kuzaku began.

Momohina went, "Ta-daaaah!" and pulled the feather bundle from the pot. The feather bundle was glistening and wet.

"Oil?" Shihoru whispered.

"Bingo! We have a winnerrrrrr!" Momohina clapped in a way that seemed dodgy as she slowly swayed the feather bundle around.

"Oil?" Merry tilted her head. "You're going to burn him?"

"Eek!" Honey Den's whole body went rigid.

Setora looked around the hold. "Will the ship be all right?"

Hold on, you two, your thinking is way too merciless.

Haruhiro cleared his throat. "If we burn him, won't he kind of die?"

"Ah!" Yume clapped her hands. "Yume thinks she's got it! It's ticklin' time, isn't it?!"

"Hahah!" Momohina's face brimmed with a smile as she pointed the feather bundle towards Yume. "Ding, ding, ding, ding, diiiing! You got it! Fifty thousand points to Yumeyume!"

"Woo! Yume got it!"

Did these two have something in common, after all?

"Urgh?!" Honey Den's eyes darted about. "T-t-tickling?! H-h-h-hold on, hey..."

Momohina went, "Mweeheehee," a dirty smile on her face as she waved the feather bundle back and forth gently, approaching Honey Den.

"No, listen, I don't mind pain, but this really isn't my thing..."

"Gwahahah! Boyyyys! Strip hiiiim!"

If that was the KMW's orders, so be it. Haruhiro and the party were underlings of the K&K Pirate Company.

Haruhiro had Kuzaku and Jimmy help disrobe a struggling Honey Den. Or rather, since it would be a real pain to untie him and then tie him up again, they cut off all of his clothes except for his underwear with knives.

He wasn't exactly ripped, and he had thick body hair, so he was hard to look at. The girls, with the exception of Momohina, looked away in distaste, but Honey Den seemed not so much embarrassed as shy and pleased.

He was a deviant. They had themselves a sexual deviant here.

"Are we ready to go full speed aheeeaaad?!" the KMW cried.

Haruhiro, Kuzaku, and Jimmy just answered, "Sure."

"You have no energyyyy! Full speed aheeeaaad?!"

While wondering what kind of ritual this was, Haruhiro desperately screamed, "Full speed ahead!"

Jimmy said, "Sure," like before, and Kuzaku shouted, "Full speed ahead!" even louder than Haruhiro.

Now the company's KMW was satisfied. "'Kay! That'll do! Let's get starteeeed. Prepare yourseeeelf!"

"No, stop, stop, stop, stop!" Honey Den howled.

"I will not stop! Meow!"

"Eh?!"

"How do you like it heeeere?!"

"Hah?! Hahaha?!"

"Moooore!"

"Nwahahhoah?! Gyahahahahahahahahahoh?! S-s-s-stop it, please?!"

"I. Will. Not. Stop. More, more! Goochie, goochie, goo!"

"Ngahhhhhhhhhhhh?! No, no, not theeeere, ahhhh?!"

"Here's the spoooot! You like it heeere, huuuuh! Here, here, here, here, here."

"Nnnghiiiiiiiiiiiaaaaaaaaaahoahhhhhhhh?!"

This was reeeeaaaally...hard to watch.

But it was wildly effective.

Honey Den finally acknowledged he had been talked into going to the dragon's nest by Red-Eyed Ben. They had wanted a younger hand along for labor, so they'd brought Step.

Relying on a map made a really long time ago by the famous adventurer Edgmer, they'd tried the route through the forest to the dragon's nest. However, they'd been found by the runaruka. After a chase in which Step was shot and killed, Ben and Honey Den had barely managed to shake their runaruka pursuers somehow.

Honey Den had learned from that, and suggested they abandon the plan. But Ben had stubbornly refused to accept it, and threatened to kill Honey Den if he backed out.

"He was serious," Honey Den told them. "He's a liar, but when he says he'll do something, he damn well does it, that bastard."

They had been together in the Skull Pirate Gang, so Honey Den knew Red-Eyed Ben well. According to Honey Den, when Ben snapped, you never knew what he'd do. The reason he'd angered Dead Skull and gotten demoted was that he'd fought with one of his fellow pirates over something petty, then later ambushed and killed the man. He told tall tales and came across as a petty thug, so people were prone to taking him lightly, but he was a capable man.

So Ben and Honey Den had stared at the map and chosen a route north along the coast for their second attempt.

It had gone well at first, with no encounters with runaruka, to the point that they were laughing, *What was that first attempt? Step died for nothing!*

However, at that point, they were almost at the dragons' nest.

Even the famous adventurer Edgmer had never entered the dragons' nest. Looking at their copy of the map, the dragons' nest was blank. The real map held nothing but a cutesy dragon and dragon eggs drawn in.

Basically, what it was like and what creatures inhabited the place was a complete unknown.

An unexplored frontier.

One that was to be, to say the least, a far more terrifying place than Honey Den had ever imagined.

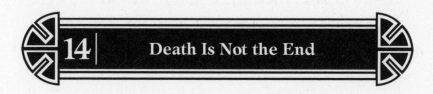

14 | Death Is Not the End

THERE WERE MANY SMALL HOLES in the rocky wall that rose high along the coast.

The seabirds apparently nested here during the spring mating season, but there was no way they had dug those themselves.

There were no holes to be seen lower on the wall, with them only appearing around seven to eight meters above the surface, so it was hard to imagine they were the result of erosion by seawater.

Had the sea breeze, or rain water, or something like that gouged out these holes over a long period of time? Haruhiro didn't know. It was a mystery.

Soon, night would come.

Haruhiro climbed up the rock wall, clinging right next to the holes.

When he looked down from the rock wall, he saw that his comrades, the K&K company's KMW Momohina, Section Chief Jimmy, Managing Director Giancarlo, and the runaruka pirate Tsiha were all looking up at him. So was Honey Den, who was bound and gagged.

He wasn't especially afraid of heights, but he was quite high, and there were rocks down below. If he messed up and fell, he'd get hurt badly. Merry was here, though, so if he didn't die instantly, he'd be all right. He just had to be sure not to strike his head. Yeah. It was fine, just fine.

Stretching his neck out, he quietly peeked into one of the holes, which had a diameter of about 1.2 meters.

It was maybe 1.5 meters deep. This hole had likely witnessed the drama of seabirds building their nests, laying eggs, and then the chicks growing large enough to leave the nest. There were feathers and nest materials scattered around, and in the middle of them— or rather, on top of them—a single man was snoring loudly.

His feet were turned this way, so it wasn't possible to make a facial confirmation. But not many people would be coming out here, three to four kilometers from Roronea, to find a place to sleep.

It was more or less certain. This man was Red-Eyed Ben, AKA Benjamin Fry.

According to the testimony of Honey Den, even after the sinking of the *Great Tiger-go,* Ben had been targeted by the dragons for days. However, perhaps because of his devilishly good luck, he had somehow managed to escape from danger.

Ben and Honey Den had been seeking a way out of the Emerald Archipelago. However, partly due to the uproar surrounding the dragons, right now, it was hard to find any ship willing to take men with reputations as bad as theirs aboard. The two had considered stowing away, but if they were caught, they'd get the stuffing beat out of them, and it wouldn't end there. They'd likely be cast into the sea. If that happened, the odds of survival were minimal.

Honey Den had despaired and turned to drinking heavily in the emergency marketplace, but Ben hadn't given up. With this hidey hole as his base of operations, he'd sought out old associates—certified deadbeats, the lowest of the low, even among pirates—and threatened them, buttered them up, deceived them, and tried to find a way to get himself on a boat.

That was going to end today. But how to end it?

According to Honey Den, Ben had hidden the treasure, and its location remained unknown. It was too big for him to keep it hidden beneath his clothes, so if he were to carry it with him, it would have to be inside a bag or something. That was what he'd done while they were in Roronea, but as far as Honey Den knew, ever since he'd moved his hiding place here, Ben had gone around without carrying anything.

He'd asked where the treasure was, but the response had been less than friendly.

"What, are you planning to steal it?"

He'd nearly gotten himself killed, so he'd never tried asking again.

Would the treasure be in this hole? From the looks of it, there was nothing like a bag lying around, but Ben might very well be using it as a pillow.

Before Ben and Honey Den had taken the coastal route to the dragons' nest, they'd needed to rest a night here. Ben had used this hole, while Honey Den slept in the one next to it.

In other words, Ben knew that Honey Den knew where his hideout was. Out of caution, he'd probably keep the treasure in another place entirely.

By Haruhiro's reasoning, the dragons attacking Roronea were trying to get their treasure back. He wanted to ask Ben where it was. Would the man honestly tell them?

Take a deep breath. Deeper. Deeper.

Haruhiro was pressed against the rock wall, so his feet weren't on the ground. Rather than sink into the ground, he would enter the wall. Become one with it. That was the image he used.

Stealth...

No good, huh? I feel like I should be able to enter it, but I can't. What could it be? It doesn't feel completely impossible. Is something off? It's not coming together. I'm probably almost there. The difference between almost there and there is huge, though.

Am I in a slump, after all? What should I do in times like this? I could do it normally before. I should be able to. There's no way I can't. It's weird that I can't. The more I think that, the more I panic. Calm down. Take a different tack. Well, it's one thing to say that to myself, but it's another thing to do it.

His comrades down below must have been thinking, *Huh, what is Haruhiro doing?*

Haruhiro couldn't waste time. He couldn't slip into it smoothly, but it wasn't like he couldn't use Stealth at all.

Fine, let's do this.

Once his mind was made up, he didn't hesitate. Haruhiro went into the hole, making hardly a sound. Ben was still snoring.

Haruhiro drew his dagger with his right hand. Then, suddenly, he took a kick to the right leg.

"Guh...!"

Taking repeated kicks as he faltered, Haruhiro was nearly forced out of the hole. He instinctively braced himself with his left hand and both legs to hold on.

Red-Eyed Ben. This guy, he wasn't sleeping. He'd been awake. Since when?

"Gahhhh!" Ben sat up, trying to take another kick at Haruhiro.

Haruhiro shouted, "Dammit!" He thrust out with his dagger.

Ben pulled his foot back. "Who the hell're you?!"

He was feeling around for something. The treasure? No. A curved sword.

In a cramped crouching position inside the hole, Ben swung the curved sword's sheathe away. He turned its cutting edge towards Haruhiro.

"I asked, who're you?! Answer me, you scallywag!"

Haruhiro said nothing. In the current situation, it was best to provide Ben with as little information as possible. Still, the hole was tight. Ben had the advantage, being deeper inside it.

Haruhiro decided to get out of the hole.

"Hey, you...!" Ben shouted.

Haruhiro didn't go far from the hole, circling around to the opposite direction from which he'd come, and waited for the man there.

"Ha...!" Yume started to shout for him.

Haruhiro looked down and shook his head.

Yume hurriedly covered her mouth with both hands.

Ben was taking his time to come out.

Don't think, Haruhiro told himself. *Not about what Ben's like, or what he'll do when he comes out. If something happens while I'm thinking, it'll slow down my reaction. For now, deal with him when he comes out. That's all I have to do.*

Eventually, Ben poked his head out. He was facing the opposite direction from Haruhiro.

"Nnngh!" Honey Den made noise through his gag.

Ben noticed, and looked down. "You..."

"Nnnnnngh...!"

Is Honey Den trying to tell Ben something? I can't tell, but Ben's shocked. Now's the time.

Haruhiro jumped on Ben. First he stabbed the dagger into Ben's shoulder, tangled with him, made it so they fell into the hole together, and then grappled with him.

"You little piece of crap, what do you think you're doing?! That hurts, dammit!"

"Where's the egg?!" Haruhiro shouted.

"Damn your mouth, Honey Den! It's not here, you idiot!"

"I'll bet! What hole did you hide it in?!"

"I dunno!"

With the dagger still buried in his right shoulder, Ben couldn't use his right arm properly. He let go of his curved sword. Haruhiro wanted to choke him out. If he were unconscious, the rest would be easy.

"Now's the time!" Haruhiro shouted. "If you talk, I'll let you go!"

"You think you're in a position to say that?! I don't even know who you are, kid! Don't act so full of yourself!"

Haruhiro didn't think he was acting full of himself. If anything, he was desperate. This man, he was strong. That, and he stank...

What *was* that? It was awful. He was beyond stinking. Was it his armpits? It was impossible to tell where the stench came from. Even if he tried not to breathe through his nose, Haruhiro could detect the strong smell. Just grappling with the guy was enough to make it unbearable. It was driving him nuts.

"You stink!" Haruhiro shouted. "Seriously!"

"Wahahahahahahaha!"

Oops.

Until that point, Ben had tried to throw Haruhiro off him, or tried to poke him in the eyes, but now he must have decided his stench was a weapon. He got really damn close.

This is terrible. I want to puke. It's mind-numbing. This guy is dead. I swear I'm going to kill him. He stinks too bad to let live.

"Guuuuuuaaaaahhhhhhhhhhhhhhhhhhhhh!"

Haruhiro mustered all his strength and slammed Ben up against the wall. He bashed Ben's head into the wall repeatedly. Ben screamed as he struck back. Up, and down.

Haruhiro took a hit in the solar plexus, and it hurt badly. Oh, crap. He got flipped over and pinned, and now his head was outside the hole.

"Screw you! Screw you! Screw you!" Ben was strangling him. With both hands. He could clench his right hand, too, apparently.

Was it a burst of hysterical strength in a time of crisis? Ben's eyes weren't just reddish brown; they were blood red. He was dripping snot and spittle, too.

Gross, Haruhiro wanted to moan. *I can't take this anymore. This is the worst.*

At the foot of the rock wall, his comrades were all shouting. Haruhiro grasped the hilt of the dagger, and stabbed into Ben's shoulder.

"Aghhhh, it huuuuuuuuurts!!"

Ben's right hand loosened its grip. Haruhiro tried to slip free, but Ben was having none of that. They were both desperate. Haruhiro was on the verge of suffocation, so he was fighting for his life.

The next thing he knew, he was falling.

"Ohhhh?! Damn you! Ohhh! Ohhhhhhhhhhhhhhh?!"

Ben was trying to point Haruhiro's body downwards. He meant to use Haruhiro as a cushion to save himself.

Am I going to die this time? No, no, no. I'm the younger one. Is it because I'm younger? Haruhiro didn't really understand, but that was what he thought. *I'm still young. I can't die.*

Maybe that thought gave him the strength, or maybe it didn't.

"Ahhhhhhhhhhhhhhhhhhhhhhhhhhhhhhhhhhhh!!" He twisted around, and left the rest to luck.

He heard a crunching, breaking sound.

Ben was beneath Haruhiro, his eyes wide. His jaw was slack, and his mouth open.

Haruhiro knew he wasn't unharmed himself, but he wanted to get away from this man as soon as possible. He tried to stand, but intense pain shot through his body, and he let out a scream despite himself.

Maybe I'm not just not unharmed, but really badly harmed? Like, huh? My consciousness is fading...

If Merry hadn't raced over to cast Sacrament, who knew what might have happened.

It was too late for Ben. There was heavy damage to his head, back, and probably internal organs, too. He died nearly instantly.

"Uwahhh," Haruhiro mumbled. "What now...?"

He crouched down and clutched his head. Honey Den had warned him that Ben was tough, but he'd underestimated the guy. Who knew he'd be so stubborn? Or, more importantly, that he'd stink that bad.

"The location of the egg..." Shihoru murmured.

That was all Shihoru said.

Sorry. Try to understand.

Everyone sighed, frowned, or stared off into space.

Yeah, I know...

In the middle of all that, Kuzaku crouched down next to Haruhiro. "Yeah," he said with a nod. "Still, I'm glad. You nearly gave me a heart attack for a moment there. You're still alive, at least. That's the most important thing. Well, we'll work something out. We always have before."

Then Kuzaku added, "Okay!"

He grabbed Haruhiro's arm, and stood up dragging Haruhiro with him.

"Let's look! I'm sure it's gotta be in one of these holes. There are a lot of holes, but there're a lot of us, too. I'm sure we'll find it in no time."

Are you an angel? was what Haruhiro wanted to ask him, but he felt like it would be misunderstood. He was too big to be an angel, anyway. Maybe size had nothing to do with it.

Haruhiro sniffled. "You sure are positive, Kuzaku, man."

"It's thanks to you, and to everyone."

"You're able to say these things so easily..."

"What things?"

"No, it's nothing."

There might not be countless holes in the rock wall, but there were dozens, maybe about a hundred. What was more, they had no proof Red-Eyed Ben had hidden the treasure in one of the holes. That said, they had no idea where else it could be. For now, they would have to try checking the holes one by one.

"We're climbing up there?" Managing Director Giancarlo objected. "You've gotta be kidding..."

"Yeah," he muttered, but he was quick to start clambering up the wall. KMW Momohina the kung-fu master mage seemed like she could walk up walls if she put her mind to it, so there were no problems there. Meanwhile, Jimmy and Tsiha decided to stay on the ground and guard Honey Den.

Shihoru stayed with Jimmy and Tsiha, while Haruhiro, Kuzaku, Yume, Merry, Setora, and Kiichi each went on checking the holes one by one.

With seven people and one pet on the job, it obviously still took a fair amount of time, but it might not have been an unbearable amount of work. It felt like Kiichi might do the work of two to three people on his own.

When they had been searching the holes for a while, Shihoru informed them the dragons were flying in.

Taking a look, Haruhiro saw that she was right; there were indeed three dragons circling over Roronea.

The dragons had descended on Roronea again yesterday, leveling a few buildings. If they found the treasure, like it was lying out somewhere, would the dragons take it back, and leave everything settled? That would be up to how the dragons felt, he supposed.

When they kept searching the holes, someone called up to them. "Hey! Hey!"

It was unquestionably Shihoru's voice. But shouting "hey" like that? It just wasn't like Shihoru. Had something happened?

Haruhiro broke off the search, leaning out from the hole. Shihoru was pointing in the direction of Roronea.

"Th-th-the dragons...!"

"Huh? The dragons...?"

What was she on about?

Looking in the direction of Roronea, wasn't one of the drag-ons that had been circling over the city heading their way now?

"O-oh, crap..." Haruhiro gasped. "This is bad, right? Huh? Wh-what do we do?"

"For now, we pull out!" Jimmy shouted.

The man slapped Tsiha on the back, and kicked Honey Den in the butt. He grabbed Shihoru by the sleeve, saying, "Come on!" as he pulled. "Everyone, get in the holes! I think we're probably the ones in danger!"

In the holes? Was that okay? Would it be all right? Jimmy, Shihoru, Tsiha, and Honey Den were running as fast as they could.

Haruhiro looked to the dragon. It was just one, and didn't seem that fast. But then, even one was dangerous enough, and it wasn't slow. Or rather, it was damn fast. Haruhiro hurried deeper into the hole.

The dragon was coming. He could sense its presence, the sound of it. It screeched loudly, and the sound echoed. He felt wind, too.

Was this the sound of its wings beating? Perhaps it was trying to land. That was the sense he got.

Where's the dragon?

Has it landed already?

What is it doing?

It's moving—I think...?

It bothered him. It wasn't so much curiosity he felt, as it was concern for whether Shihoru was safe.

If Shihoru was being targeted by the dragon, he had to save her. If he drew its attention and then hid out in the hole, the dragon couldn't come in. Probably. Well, there had to be some-thing he could do.

Haruhiro got down on all fours and poked his head out.

The dragon was there.

Right beneath the hole where Haruhiro was.

It was doing something on the rocks.

It was big. Its wings were folded now, but it still had to be more than twenty meters long.

Emeralds. It was like its whole body was actually covered in emeralds. Beautiful. It was unbelievably pretty. It was hard to think of it as a living creature. But it was moving. What was it doing with its head lowered, like a dog sniffing for something?

Haruhiro didn't see Shihoru and the others. Had they hidden somewhere?

He pulled his head back in. The dragon went to spread its wings.

It was scary. He backed away. Retreated. Haruhiro backed off to the very bottom of his hole.

The dragon flew. It wasn't just noise and wind. As the dragon ascended, for just a moment, he saw it with his own eyes. It had been almost right beneath him, so it was passing by the hole Haruhiro was in.

This was no wyvern. Like birds, wyverns' front legs had devel-oped into wings. The dragons of the Emerald Archipelago had wings on their backs and separate front legs, even if those weren't as strong as their hind legs. In fact, they were less like front legs, and more like arms.

Maybe the dragon was holding something in its hands?

The dragon cried loudly once again. It happened immediately after that.

Whoosh! Something fell at an incredible speed. Then, afterwards, there was a splat, or maybe not.

Had the dragon thrown whatever it was? The thing it had in its hands before.

The dragon went quiet.

Where was the dragon? Had it left? Or was it still up there?

Haruhiro hesitated for a good long while, then stuck his body out from the hole as little as possible, first checking above him. Not there. They were over Roronea. How many? One, two...three. It looked like that dragon had already left, and had returned to the group.

"Shihoru...?! Shihoru!" Haruhiro got out of the hole and climbed down the rock wall. Before he had fully descended, Shihoru, Jimmy, Tsiha, and even Honey Den rushed over.

The four had run as far as they could, hiding themselves in a low place among the rocks. Thanks to that, they were safe. Which likely meant the dragon had never been interested in Shihoru and the rest to begin with.

Momohina and Giancarlo, as well as Kuzaku, Yume, Merry, Setora, and Kiichi, came out of their holes and down the rock wall.

"What *was* that?" Haruhiro muttered, then, *Ulp.* He covered his mouth. It was clear what it was.

There were scraps of meat, bone, what looked like organs, and blood splattered all over the rocks.

Come to think of it, I killed him. That thought occurred to him too late. If he hadn't done it, he'd have died himself, so what choice had he had?

Could this be the first time he'd killed a human being? It wasn't a good feeling, but honestly, he didn't feel all that guilty. He'd taken a whole lot of lives before. Maybe it just meant that he wasn't so pure that his victim happening to be human this time was going to make him feel pangs of conscience.

Red-Eyed Ben. Benjamin Fry had been a uniquely wretched piece of scum. Though, seeing him reduced to the point where he was unrecognizable, even if Haruhiro didn't feel bad for the guy, he did feel a sense of ephemerality.

Honey Den must have been shocked, because he sat there, staring at what had once been Red-Eyed Ben.

Haruhiro shook his head lightly, sighing once. "I wonder if the dragons followed his stench?"

"They wanted revenge, but he was already dead, so the dragon took out its frustrations. Is that what you mean?" Giancarlo mused with a shrug. "Well, if they're satisfied now, then good..."

"I don't know about that." Jimmy pointed towards Roronea.

The dragons were descending.

"Foo?" Yume tilted her head to the side.

"Nyo?" Momohina narrowed her eyes. "Aroro? That's north of the town, isn't it?"

"North, but—" Kuzaku was speechless.

Giancarlo took off running. "I'll go take a look! If the emergency market gets hit now, it won't be pretty!"

Grimgar
of
Fantasy and Ash

15 | Negotiator

THERE WERE NO STALLS, no shops, no nothing. Everything was smashed.

Humans, orcs, and a variety of other races—all of them were collapsed and covered in blood. Many were crushed, or had a piece of their body torn off. There were arms, legs, even heads rolling around. They must never have imagined the dragons would descend on this emergency market.

Hey, that's weird, they're coming this way! By the time someone had shouted that, it was already too late.

This tragedy really wasn't pretty.

The three dragons had already flown off, and they were circling in the air above Roronea.

"We have to help the living," Merry said.

They thought that sounded reasonable, so they split up and went to search for survivors, but then the dragons descended again, and everything went to hell.

Haruhiro and his party weren't safe in town, so they'd have to evacuate to the dense forest. But was the forest safe? There was no guarantee the dragons wouldn't come into the forest, so they might be forced to fight them. They started resolving themselves to do just that, but the dragons never did come into the forest.

It looked like a lot of people had fled into Roronea from the emergency market. The dragons now focused their attention on them. Smoke was rising from all over town, and screams could faintly be heard coming from the town, even in the forest.

Ultimately, up until the dragons flew off after noon, all Haruhiro and his companions could do was hold their breaths as they hid in the forest.

They started looking for survivors in the emergency market afterward, but could find none left breathing. As they were looking, the dragons came back, so they ended up hurriedly fleeing into the forest once more.

The dragons were apparently coming back from their fishing grounds where they'd eaten. They'd wreaked havoc in Roronea on full stomachs, and then returned to their nests when evening came.

That being the case, it wasn't until night that the extent of the damage became clear.

Extensive was the only way to describe it. There were over eighty people just among the confirmed dead, and more than another three hundred wounded.

From what Haruhiro and the rest heard, there was no small number of people who had made a mad dash through the streets only to jump into the sea from the piers and wharves. Because of that, the damage to the port was especially heavy. The No. 1, No. 3, and No. 4 piers were thoroughly destroyed, and the No. 1 and No. 2 wharves were heavily damaged, so the only one still reasonably intact was the No. 5 Pier.

The storehouses near the port were also smashed by the dragons, and a large quantity of grains, salted meat, fish, pickled vegetables, fruit, and liquor had been spoiled.

It was a crippling blow to Roronea. And the dragons might still return the next day.

When the sun set, the pirates began fighting over money, food, and water. There were desperate pirates who picked a fight with whoever they could, too. The boats staying offshore rushed to the No. 5 Pier out of fear of the dragons, and the heavy traffic led to utter chaos.

In order to control the pirates, Giancarlo, Momohina, and Jimmy ran all over, but even once the clouds that had hung low over the town since afternoon began to pour rain, the town showed no sign of quieting.

No good was going to come of staying in Roronea in this point, and it was just dangerous. In the middle of the rain, Haruhiro and the party pulled out and went to the rock wall from earlier.

The runaruka pirate Tsiha came along with them.

At the rock wall, Honey Den was delighted to see them return. "Mmpf, mmpf, mmpf, mmpf!" he shouted.

No, he might not have been delighted, but since he had his hands bound behind his back, a gag in his mouth, both knees and ankles tied together with rope, and a rope around his waist tied to an outcropping on a boulder, he must have been at least a little relieved.

He might be hungry, and it had started raining, so he was certainly in a less than pleasant situation. Still, seeing the way he refused to stop incessantly going, "Mmpf, mmpf, mmpf, mmpf!" Honey Den was still doing relatively well.

Why had they come back to the rock wall? One reason was that they had left Honey Den here when they returned to Roronea. The emergency situation had left them no other choice, but it wasn't as if Haruhiro didn't feel it was a little cruel, and he'd have trouble sleeping at night if they just left the guy like this.

Undoing just the rope around his waist and the bonds on his legs, they took Honey Den somewhere out of the rain. There was a convenient cave not far away, so they decided to rest there.

No one had much to say. Kuzaku asked permission to lie down, and he was asleep in no time.

Honey Den was getting irritating with his muffled cries, so Haruhiro undid his gag and just listened to his pitiful begging for food. When he gave the man some of their portable rations, he finally shut up.

It was getting brighter outside. The rain hadn't let up. According to Tsiha, on days when it rained, the dragons tended not to leave their nest. If that was the case, they could catch their breaths.

Haruhiro stood up with some effort. "The night's over, so I'd say it's about time we went out searching."

"Still, we don't know what hole it's in, right?" Setora asked. "Worse yet, it might well not even be here."

Setora might be right. But she also might be wrong.

Haruhiro looked from the entrance of the cave towards the rocks outside. The rain should have washed a lot of it away, so they couldn't find his remains easily, but when Haruhiro had asked Red-Eyed Ben, whose life had ended here, where the treasure was, the response had been, *It's not here, you idiot.*

I'll bet. Haruhiro believed the dead man.

Thinking about it, it was a mystery. He'd been careless and addle-brained, and frankly Ben had had every reason to call him an idiot.

Benjamin Fry hadn't been an honest man, by any means. He'd easily deceived others, tricking them with quickly improvised lies. That was the kind of man he had been. If he'd said something was white, it was best to start off assuming it was black.

"If it's not here, it's not here, and we'll work from there," Haruhiro said. "For now, everyone stay here. I can do this alone."

Haruhiro left the cave. It wasn't visible from a distance, but Ben's blood and flesh were still clinging to the rocks. That meant it was just above here.

He carefully climbed the rock wall, which was slick with rain. When he reached the hole in question, the inside was close to pitch black. Well, he'd manage somehow.

Moving aside pieces of wood and branches that seabirds had brought as material for their nests, along with other objects he couldn't identify, he searched.

Was it his imagination? He occasionally smelt the dead man's stench. That man had slept here. His head had rested right around here, and—

His back. No, his waist would have been around here. When Red-Eyed Ben had lain down to sleep, his butt would have been right around here.

The ground was soft. Or more like there was an indentation to begin with. Ben had dug it out, and then laid down branches and whatever on top of it.

When Haruhiro cleared those away, he found it.

It was there.

A bag made from thick hemp, or a similar material.

He pulled the bag out. He opened it. Haruhiro gulped, and then threw up a bit.

"This is it," he whispered. He closed the bag and shouldered it.

When he left the hole, Kuzaku, Merry, Setora, and Kiichi were down below. Yume, Shihoru, and Tsiha were probably guarding Honey Den.

"Found it," Haruhiro said.

"Huh..." said Merry.

"Nyaa?" Kiichi put in.

"What did you say?" Setora asked.

Kuzaku was slack-jawed. "For real?"

Everyone was surprised. Haruhiro was surprised in many ways, too.

What an idiot he had been. He should have immediately assumed that if Red-Eyed Ben said it wasn't there, the opposite was true, and it actually was. If a man as suspicious as him was going to hide something, where would it be? The hole where he was staying was obviously the most suspicious place.

Haruhiro descended the rock wall, and returned to the cave with Kuzaku and the others. The moment he saw the bag Haruhiro was carrying, Honey Den shouted, "Ah!"

Haruhiro opened the bag again. Was the large amount of dried grass stuffed inside intended as insulation? The man had been taking good care of it, in his own way. Haruhiro brushed aside the grass.

It was glossy. A deep green. If they looked at it under sunlight, it would be a brilliant green, no doubt.

The egg. It was definitely egg-shaped. Taken at its widest point, it might have a diameter of about twenty centimeters. It wasn't small, but it felt like an egg from those dragons could have been bigger.

Haruhiro tried flicking it with a finger. It was hard. Like a rock. It wasn't going to scratch easily.

He tried lifting it.

"Heavy..."

It really was a rock. It was heavy like one.

Merry put a hand on the egg, closing her eyes. "It's very cold. It may be a genuine egg, but I wouldn't expect it to hatch."

"Is it petrified or something?" Shihoru asked, looking more at Merry's expression than at the egg.

"Could be." Merry opened her eyes. She hurriedly pulled her hand back. "I wouldn't really know. That was just the feeling I got."

Kuzaku crossed his arms and nodded. "That means we can't eat it, right?"

"You want to eat it?" Haruhiro asked, mind-boggled.

But Kuzaku turned to him with all seriousness and replied, "Huh? Wouldn't you want to try it?"

"No, not really."

"Ohhhh. Well, that's just how you are, after all. You're pretty conservative about what you're willing to eat."

"I'm not sure that's the issue here...?"

"Listen, that thing is worth five thousand gold, people." Honey Den sounded like he had bitten into something unpleasant.

"Fwoo..." Yume twisted her neck around. "Five thousand? Mmmm?"

"*Gold?*"

Haruhiro nearly dropped the egg in surprise, and Kuzaku went "Whoa," and jumped back and away from it.

"F-five thousand! Five thousand gold?! That's a whole ladda money! I'm not sure what a ladda is supposed to be, though..."

"That's what Ben told me, at least," Honey Den said. "I dunno if it's true. Even a hundred gold would be enough to make us set for life. That was the plan, at least..."

Honey Den's shoulders slumped, and he started muttering curses. In a way, it was impressive to see that he was so scummy, he could still bemoan his misfortune at this stage of the game.

"You realize a whole lot of people are dead thanks to you two, right?" Haruhiro snapped.

"Wasn't my idea. Besides, even if I didn't help, I'm sure Ben'd have done it alone. He's the one to blame. If not for him, none of this would ever've happened. Am I right, or what?"

"What do you mean, 'Am I right, or what?'" Setora turned a cold gaze towards Honey Den.

Kiichi was glaring threateningly at the man desperately in need of dental care, too.

"Haru, we're done with him," Setora said freezingly. "Wouldn't it be best to finish him off? He'll be in our way, and he's evil."

"D-don't be like that!" Honey Den yelped. "I-I may not look it, but I can be useful, okay?"

"I can't imagine you would be," she sneered.

"No, I mean it! That's why Ben brought me in on this!"

"Did you not just say he could have done it himself?"

"Th-that was just, uh, you know, a figure of speech, okay?"

Were they done with him, or not? It was a hard call. Even if they were, Haruhiro didn't see a need to kill him, but he didn't want to be stuck looking at the guy's face much longer, either. What to do?

"Tsiha, this thing, you ever see one before?" Haruhiro asked, just to be sure.

Tsiha looked at the egg in silence for a while, then shook his head. "No," he said at last. "But probably dragon egg. To dragon, give back good. Not give back, dragon stay angry."

"How do you think we should go about givin' it back?" Yume arched her eyebrows and hugged her knees. "The dragons, they're hollerin' mad, you know? Like, imagine Yume were to take them the egg, right? Yume, she'd get gobbled up by the dragons, don't you think?"

"Why don't we just leave it out somewhere?" Kuzaku suggested, then whacked himself two to three times in the head. "No good, huh? Wait, is it no good? I dunno, but either way, I have a feeling they won't stop attacking the town. They've totally snapped."

"We can't take the ship out anymore, either..." Shihoru looked outside the cave, sighing deeply.

"Give it back, huh...?" Haruhiro murmured to himself.

"Give it back..." Kuzaku parroted back, looking up to the ceiling of the cave.

"Give it back...?" Yume tilted her head to the side ninety degrees. "If Yume had to return a thing to someone, do you think she'd go to them?"

"Go to them..." Merry tucked in her chin and looked down. "To the dragons' nest?"

"I...I don't wanna!" Honey Den screamed and tried to run out of the cave.

Setora immediately swept his leg and tripped him. The rock surface was far from flat here, so Honey Den let out a squeal as his face got all scratched up.

"N-no, I don't wanna go there," the pirate moaned. "If it means going to that place again, I'd rather die. No, that's going a little far. I can't die until I've slept with a whole lot of good women, and eaten sweet stuff until my cheeks caved in..."

"What is *with* this guy?" Setora was past being put off, and was shuddering a little.

Seriously, though, what *was* with him?

If they left him alone, Honey Den seemed likely to crawl out of the cave on his belly, so Haruhiro planted a foot on his back for lack of a better alternative.

"Gyauagh?! You inhuman monsteeeeer!"

"Oh, shut up... Also, I don't want to hear that from *you*."

"Then let me go. Set me free. If you do, I'll remember you as a saint."

"Mind your manners. Do you want to get fed to the dragons?"

"I-I'm sorry, i-it won't happen again, forgive me, please, have mercy..."

Even just stepping on him like this, Haruhiro felt his heart being dirtied a little more each second. But if he removed his foot, this man was more or less guaranteed to make a run for it.

"You say you never want to go there again, but you never went in there in the first place, right?" Haruhiro demanded. "Red-Eyed Ben went into the nest alone, and he managed to come back in one piece."

"That bastard was a little weird. In the head, you know. Me, I'm sane..."

"You know the way there, right?"

"Only the way there. There's no map once you get past that point, either. Going in there, it's not something that a sane man does."

"But, Haru." Setora looked at Honey Den as she might look at a pile of excrement.

You don't have to look at him, Haruhiro couldn't help but think. *Not many guys are as worthless as this.*

"Do we have any obligation to go so far?" Setora asked. "Now that we've found the egg, I think we can say we have uncovered the reason the dragons are attacking Roronea. Our jobs should be done at this point."

"You're right, Setora," Haruhiro said. "It's exactly as you say, but..."

The rain was still coming down. Had it let up a little? Would the dragons fly today? What was happening to the ships that'd rushed to the No. 5 Pier? Most of them probably couldn't leave. It wasn't just the rain; the wind was strong, too. The seas were rough.

Roronea was a pirate town. The supplies they went through mostly came by ship. If shipping was no longer viable, the populace would starve in no time. Would they fish to eat? They could try hunting in the forest, too, but the runarukas wouldn't stand for it.

What Haruhiro had to keep in mind was that this problem didn't only affect the islanders anymore. The party was here on this island. It affected them, too.

They should meet with Giancarlo, or Jimmy. Haruhiro wanted to hear the runarukas' opinions, too. He decided to have Tsiha call his elder brother Mwadan, the next in line to become chief of the tribe.

Kuzaku said he'd go with Tsiha, and Haruhiro ran all the way to Roronea to find Giancarlo.

The town had been laid to waste. It was best to assume anyone out in the streets was a looter. When he snuck his way through to the port, there were still several ships moored to the No. 5 Pier, and a crowd had gathered. They were arguing pretty loudly about something.

When he got closer, Giancarlo was shouting at the pirates, and they were shouting back. It could turn to fisticuffs at any moment.

When Momohina got in the middle of them, the pirates bowed down immediately. It looked like things had been solved peaceably.

Jimmy was there, too.

Haruhiro tried talking to him. "Section Chief."

"Oh. You, huh? Good to see you're still alive."

"You look exhausted," Haruhiro told him. "Are you okay?"

"I'm undead; it comes with the territory. Did you have something to talk about?"

Haruhiro whispered a report about how they'd found the egg. Then it was decided not just Jimmy but also Momohina would come with them to confirm they had the genuine object, and from there, they'd discuss what would happen next.

Not long after they left Roronea, the dragons took flight in spite of the rain.

If the dragons smashed the No. 5 Pier, too, they'd seriously be out of ways to leave the island. No, Haruhiro wasn't optimistic enough to think that it couldn't happen. He expected it probably would.

Giancarlo and his people had half given up. It might have been that they were exhausted, but even when they saw the dragons, they didn't act particularly surprised, or act like they were worried for their future prospects.

Tsiha and Kuzaku had returned with Mwadan by the time they arrived. Mwadan was pretty angry at Honey Den, and said he should be offered as a sacrifice in some sort of ritual, but they got him to hold off on that for the moment.

First of all, they had to decide what was to be done with the dragon egg. Mwadan thought it should be returned to where it rightfully belonged.

"Whether this is dragon egg or not, I do not know," Mwadan said. "However, it is important to dragons. No question. Runarukas punish thieves. Person who stole, made to return things. Things they stole, returned to where they came from. Then punishment. You humans do same. Dragons do same. Return stolen things. No other choice."

"I more or less agree," Giancarlo said, raising his hand. "Well, we won't know if that solves things or not until we try it. It seems that's the only way we can show the dragons our sincere contrition."

"Mewwww. Let's do iiiiit!" Momohina turned to Haruhiro, and stretched both hands out towards him. "Okay!"

Haruhiro responsively said, "Okay," and placed his left hand on top of Momohina's palm. Was he doing this right?

"Nooo. That's not it! Give me the dragon's eggy-weggy!"

"Oh..."

He wasn't sure she should be calling it that, but Haruhiro passed Momohina the egg, bag and all.

But was this okay?

Haruhiro looked to Shihoru. When he was in a bind, he always looked to Shihoru for salvation. It had totally become a habit. Shihoru looked Haruhiro in the eye and nodded.

"Nngh! Eggy-weggy!" Momohina urged him.

Haruhiro pulled the bag back just before he would have placed it on Momohina's palms.

"No."

"Nyo?"

"I can't hand it over. We haven't received our reward yet."

"About that…" Giancarlo started to say, but Haruhiro interrupted him with an, "I know."

"This isn't a situation where you can send out a boat to take us to Vele," Haruhiro said. "Right? More than that, if we don't do something about the dragons, we don't know what will happen tomorrow."

Giancarlo frowned and shrugged.

Haruhiro kept pushing. "We're happy to help you with returning the egg to the dragons' nest. However, we're going to need more of a reward. The K&K Pirate Company is raking it in, right? You guys have money. And by the way, from what Honey Den tells us, a dragon egg is apparently worth five thousand gold coins."

Grimgar
of
Fantasy and Ash

16 | The One Who Landed

THE EAST SHORE of the island was mostly rocky beaches, while the west coast had more sandy beaches. So while it would have been shorter to travel north along the east coast, the longer west coast route was easier to walk despite being the long way around.

There were sheer cliffs at some places along the coast, and they had to enter the forest there, but Tsiha and Mwadan were accompanying them.

The Kamushika tribe that Tsiha belonged to was large in scale, and Mwadan was a famed warrior, so he was known even by other tribes. Furthermore, Tsiha's other brother Tanba was explaining the situation to all the other tribes for them. Thanks to that, they didn't have to worry about being ambushed by runarukas.

Not long after they set out, it began to rain. The roughly two-day trek to the dragons' nest was little different from going on a pleasant stroll. They even had the spare time to be excited by unusual birds, or frightened by mushrooms so bright in color that they looked poisonous.

Honey Den, whom they had brought as a guide just in case, stopped at one point and said, "From here on, it gets crazy dangerous..."

They didn't really need him to tell them that. One look at the mountain would have made anyone hesitate.

Looking at that mountain horizontally, it was more or less a table. It had a caldera, you could say. The top had probably blown off in an eruption, and it had a considerably sunken crater. There were hardly any foothills, and the surface of the mountain had a fairly steep slope. It was reasonably tall, too, so it would be hard to climb the mountain even with specialized equipment.

If not for the narrow rift opening in the side of the slope, it was likely no one would have been able to enter this mountain. And that rift was clearly dangerous, too. It was easily wide enough to permit a person entry, but it was over a hundred meters high, maybe hundreds of meters, so it felt bizarrely narrow.

What's more, it was pitch black beyond the rift, so they had absolutely no idea what it was like inside. On one hand, it felt like they could go in—or rather, there was no question that they could, physically, go inside it. But on the other hand, it felt forbidding, like they absolutely must not go in there.

Tsiha and Mwadan made no attempt to approach the rift, and were watching over Haruhiro and the party from a distance. Either way, they had the runaruka taboo against entering the nest, so this was where they had to part ways. If anything, the party could be grateful the runarukas had come this far.

Haruhiro looked up to the rift. He felt something tightening in the general area of his stomach, and he was suffering.

"It's a bit past noon now." Kuzaku looked up to the sky. "Do we attack like this?"

Momohina was already a short way inside the rift, looking around busily. "Hum, hum, hum...?"

"I-I'm not going, okay?!" Honey Den sat down on the ground. "I turned back not far inside there anyway! I wouldn't be any help!"

"I suppose we no longer need you then, do we?" Setora asked coolly.

Honey Den rapidly performed a kowtow. "Stop it! Don't talk like that! I'm begging you!"

Incidentally, this man's hands were still bound behind his back. The one time they'd undone them, he'd immediately made a break for it.

Merry seemed to be trying to see through the darkness as she carefully scrutinized the rift. Beside her, Yume, who was doing repeated stretches for exercise, went, "Nuuu," with a big stretch.

Kiichi went as far as Momohina's feet, sniffing repeatedly before making a nyaa sound.

"The dragons went out this morning." Shihoru glanced at Haruhiro.

Haruhiro nodded, and took a breath. "Shall we go?"

Giancarlo and Jimmy had remained in Roronea. As its managing director, Giancarlo had to handle the K&K Pirate

Company and keep the unruly pirates in line. Jimmy specialized in mental labor. He was more suited to assisting Giancarlo than to exploring the dragons' nest.

Momohina took point, while Haruhiro, Kuzaku, Setora and Kiichi, Merry, Shihoru, and Yume followed her into the rift, single-file, in that order. Momohina carried a lamp, while Haruhiro held the bag that contained the dragons' egg over his shoulder.

"So long, you little turds! I hope you rot!" The thick voice echoed from behind them, and when they turned back, Honey Den was hopping up and down with a smile.

"Why, you..." Setora broke into a run.

Honey Den let out a little shriek, and bolted like a startled hare. Perhaps he'd forgotten that, where he was going, Tsiha and Mwadan were waiting.

"Ohhh...?! Wait, stop, what are you doi—"

"Serves him right," Merry muttered.

What would ultimately happen to Honey Den? Well, who really cared? It was best not to think about it.

They continued through the rift. It wasn't exactly twisty, but it wasn't perfectly straight, either. The ground was fairly flat. The air was a little cold and damp. There was no wind.

"You think he was claustrophobic or something?" Kuzaku suggested.

Haruhiro was thinking along the same lines. What had Honey Den been so scared of? Up to this point, nothing had been that dangerous.

Momohina kept pushing onward.

"Did something...fall?" Shihoru raised her voice. It was true, there had been a sound other than their footsteps.

Momohina came to a stop. "Hmm?" She turned her lamp to the rear.

Kiichi let out a sharp cry, and Shihoru gulped and clung on to Merry. Somewhere between Shihoru and Yume, there was this thin, writhing thing.

Yume backed away. "A snaaaake? Maybe...?"

"I wonder..." Haruhiro squinted. It was blackish, and resembled a snake, but it was also like a bug, too. That said, it didn't have a large number of legs like a centipede or millipede, and he didn't see anything resembling legs at all, in fact. Besides, it was much bigger than a millipede, and easily over a meter in length.

"It doesn't look like a snake." Setora readied herself, glancing upwards. "If it fell from above, that means—"

Drop, drop, drop, drop, one after another, those long, thin creatures dropped down, and their screams echoed.

Even Haruhiro went, "Whoa?!"

His head. There was a creature on his head. It was pretty heavy. It felt prickly. He hurriedly jumped up, and knocked the creature off. When he did, the next one landed on his left shoulder, and his right arm. "Huaugh?!" The weird cry escaped from his mouth without his volition. What was this? They were scary, scary, scary.

Momohina shouted something even more scary. "Nyaa! They're jam-packed in here!"

Jam-packed? What'd that mean? The lamp's light wavered. It flickered off the rift walls.

223

The walls were writhing. No. Those weren't rock or stone; they were alive. They were jam-packed with long, thin creatures clinging to them.

Honey Den had told them, "Going in there, it's not something a sane man does."

It makes sense now. So this was what he was talking about. Fair enough; this is pretty bad. I want to go home.

"Gyaaaah! Don't give iiiin! Chaaaarge! Go, goooo!" Momohina hollered.

If Momohina hadn't given the order, Haruhiro might have decided to retreat. If they'd pulled out, they'd probably never have felt like entering the rift again.

Even as he felt half ready to cry, Haruhiro pushed his comrades from behind, urging them on, and pushed forward in a half frenzied state himself.

We have to go. There's no other choice. But even if we made it through this crazy, unpleasant area, how are we going to get back? Won't we have to come through here again? There's no way I want to do that.

"Gyahhhh! It went down my back!" Shihoru screamed in an incredibly terrified voice.

Haruhiro wanted to do something for her, but he had one of the creatures wrapped around his face himself. In other words, he was in a state of AHHHHHHHHHHHHHHHHHHHHHHHHHH.

What was AHHHHHHHHHHHHHHH? He didn't even know anymore.

He tripped, and crashed into the walls. When he did, those long, thin creatures were there. The place was full of them.

Suddenly, Haruhiro felt as if he had reached enlightenment. He, too, was a living creature, so wasn't this fine?

Hell no! Of course not. Not in any way! He wanted out. It wasn't supposed to be like this! He hadn't thought it through enough!

I was wrong, he thought, regretting it from the bottom of his heart. *I mean, Red-Eyed Ben was a stubborn guy, but he was just a pirate, and we're, well, you know, what? Volunteer soldiers? Or, like, experienced adventurers, you could say? He made it there and back, so, honestly, to be blunt, I can't say I didn't expect this to be easy. Well, I kind of did. It goes without saying, I warned myself against that. "Don't let your guard down," I said. "You can't take these things lightly." But, really, Red-Eyed Ben could do something, but we couldn't? It wasn't possible, right?*

It was really hard to brush away that feeling, and our money situation is really tight, so I figured if this went well and we could make a fortune, it'd make me happier about our future prospects. It was true in Roronea, and it'll be even more true at our next stop in Vele, but if we want to interact with civilization, money is a necessity. They say money makes the world go 'round. You can never have too much money. It's a problem not having any. But, well, if I hadn't been thinking we could handle it somehow, I'd never have volunteered to help. My comrades were surprisingly up for it, too. They probably figured we had this. I think maybe we all felt like that. I mean, no way, right? We'd never expect a trap like this was waiting for us.

It feels like we've been running for like fifty hours. No, it's not that long. But it feels like it's been more than two days—no—like it's been a whole lifetime? So, what, is my life over?

Haruhiro bolted towards the light, and when he leapt out the other side, it was a world of green.

Was it a forest? The trees and surface were covered with moss, or ivy, or something. It was all green.

Haruhiro was in a daze for a moment, but each time the long, thin creatures that were still wrapped around his body twitched, it was unpleasant, and prickly.

Dammit , dammit, dammit! He brushed the creatures away, freeing himself from them, and then checked that all his comrades were there.

Kuzaku was spread-eagled next to the exit to the rift, the creatures swarming around him. Was he okay? He was okay, right?

Yume and Shihoru were pulling the creatures off of each other.

Setora, who was crouched down clutching Kiichi, had another of the creatures crawling on her shoulders. When Haruhiro went over and grabbed it, throwing it away, Setora looked at him with empty eyes and said, "...Oh. Thanks. Haru. I love you."

Uh, sorry.

Momohina seemed totally fine. She'd climbed a tree covered in moss and ivy, and she was looking around the area.

Man, she's really something. What goes on in that head of hers...?

The one who seemed to have taken it the worst was Shihoru. Everyone was bruised, scraped, and cut all over, but in Shihoru's case, the mental trauma was even worse than that. She'd said it had gone down her back. Her clothes were a mess. Most likely, she had torn them herself to get rid of the creature that had gotten in there. Her clothes were in pieces. Shihoru was huddled in an indecent state, shuddering.

Haruhiro took off his cloak and draped it over Shihoru. She didn't respond. Shihoru was here in body, but it seemed her mind was somewhere else, far away. He hoped she'd come back. But maybe expecting it right now was a little much. Yeah, probably. Of course it was...

Leaving it up to Yume and Merry to care for Shihoru, Haruhiro headed over to rescue Kuzaku. Kuzaku had more than thirty of the creatures on him, and it was difficult. While he was still in the middle of helping Kuzaku get rid of them, Setora came to help.

"Forget what I said earlier," she said.

Right. Um, sorry...

Once everyone was in a state where they could move, Momohina came down from the tree and lead the party onward. It was green everywhere but the sky, so it was impossible to tell directions, but the further they got from the rift, the closer they had to be to the dragons' nest. Probably.

They went on for a little while, and came to an eerily blue pond. It was intensely suspicious, so they circled around it and kept going. There they ran into a far-too-blue river. It seemed to be a river, at least, but it wasn't flowing. It was so blue that it looked like it was painted there, which was clearly weird, so something had to be up. Still, they had to cross it to get any further. Was there no other choice?

Haruhiro volunteered and had everyone stay where they were as he went ahead and approached the blue river alone. When he was just one step away, waves formed on the river's surface, and something blue crawled out of the water.

Haruhiro came close to screaming, but he held it in, drawing his dagger as he backed away.

"Delm, hel, en, balk, zel, arve!" Momohina immediately blew it away with the Blast spell.

That was fine, but Haruhiro ended up splattered in blue liquid, chunks of flesh, and who knew what else. It was burning hot, too. He had steam rising from his whole body.

Wait, was it melting? Could it be a powerful acid? On top of that, more and more of the blue things were coming out of the river.

"Retreat! Retreeeeaaaat! Get outta there!" Momohina was shouting.

I agree that's the right course of action, but I'm burning here, you know?

However, Haruhiro couldn't just sit there and burn. He desperately crawled away as his clothes smoldered and his body melted.

Once they had gone a long way and shaken the blue things, he had Merry cast Sacrament on him. Despite as hot as it had felt, he hadn't melted as badly as he thought. Still, his clothing was full of holes.

"Ohh, sexy! Yep!" Momohina gave him a thumbs-up to try to cheer him up, but it was no consolation whatsoever.

The blue pond and river, whatever they were, seemed dangerous. They'd have to avoid them. But could they reach the dragons without crossing that river?

They investigated various possibilities, and it looked like it wouldn't be impossible to climb into the treetops and then advance by climbing from branch to branch, tree to tree. This being an unexplored frontier, not only were the trunks of the trees thick, but their branches were thick, too. Thanks to the moss, ivy, and whatnot, the branches were stuck together in places, too. It didn't look like their strength would be an issue.

That said, the treetops had their own problems. It was like walking a tightrope in some places, and there were points where they had to jump from one to the next. That, and if they fell, the blue river was below, so there were all sorts of thrills involved.

Also, they realized this a bit later, but there were a good number of monkey-like creatures here—no, creatures that were probably monkeys—and they often jumped from branch to branch. That made the branches shake, which was scary.

The *ook, ook, ook* sounds they made grated on the ears, too. It felt like they were mocking them, even if that wasn't actually the case.

In the evening, Haruhiro and the rest spotted the dragons' shadows. They had likely returned to the nest. It had gotten dark, so they decided to rest on the ground, not in the trees.

Except for Momohina. She said, "You don't always have the chance, soooo," and apparently wanted to sleep up in the trees.

Do what you want, thought Haruhiro.

Letting the thoroughly exhausted Shihoru and Kuzaku rest for a night, Haruhiro, Yume, Merry, and Setora and Kiichi took turns on watch.

Haruhiro took the first watch. The monkeys were chattering in the distance. Were they monkeys? He thought they were monkeys. Probably. They were noisy during the day, but were they active at night, too?

It was dark. No, more than that. It was almost completely black. If something tried to creep up on him, he was sure he wouldn't be able to notice. This was dangerous. But their stamina was at its limit. There was no way to move forward, not in this darkness. Should they light a fire? If they did, it would be like loudly announcing that strange people were here, so he felt like it wasn't a very good idea. He had to wait for time to pass while fighting psychological struggles like that and staying as alert as possible.

How many nights had he spent like this? He was used to it, but it was tough. It was tough, but fortunately time didn't stop. No matter how slow it felt, it was definitely flowing.

Haruhiro stuck a hand down his collar and pulled out a flat object. It was on a chain, and he always kept it around his neck. It wasn't shining now, of course. When was the last time it had? Before, the bottom portion had shone green.

That's weird, he thought.

He suddenly tried shaking it. Then he tried shaking it a few more times next to his ear. Did he hear a slight sound inside?

"Could it be broken?" he murmured.

Immediately after he said that, someone called his name—
"Haru?"—and the double shock of that surprise nearly gave him
a heart attack.

Haruhiro stuffed the receiver down his shirt in a hurry.

"Oh, you were up...?" He started to stand up, then sat back
down.

Merry sat down next to him. "I have the next watch. You sleep."

"...Yeah. That's right. I have to wonder whether I actually can
sleep, though."

"I was able to, surprisingly. I think I must be pretty dense."

"Nah, you were tired, I'm sure."

"That doesn't just go for me. Anyway, sleep. Even just lying
down will make a difference."

"Yeah," he responded, but for some reason Haruhiro didn't move.

Did he not want to move? He wondered. Merry was silent,
not urging him to go.

When he moved, his shoulder touched Merry's. They were
that close? He was surprised. His heart was beating like crazy. He
had to stay alert. Yeah. Stay alert.

"Haru," she said quietly.

I can't just stay put. It's not right.

Haruhiro leaned more fully against Merry's body. It was
like he was pressing his ear to her shoulder. He was afraid she'd
dodge to avoid him. She didn't. Merry rubbed her cheek against
Haruhiro's head.

Ohh, I want to stay like this, he thought. *I wish I could just go
to sleep this way.*

He hadn't said a word, but as if she were agreeing to his wish, Merry nodded slightly. For some reason he recalled Setora saying, "Haru. I love you," and his chest hurt. But he thought, *I love you. Merry, I love you.*

He should put it into words. That was definitely what he should do. But the moment he went to say it—

"Eeeek!" Momohina shrieked from up in the treetops.

What? Was she talking in her sleep? No. Momohina threw something down from the trees. In the area where it came down, Kuzaku cried out, "Whah?!" He jumped up, and the rest of their comrades woke one after another.

Momohina was shouting. "Look out! We may be surrounded!"

Something was attacking them. They didn't know what. It was too dark. Even so, Haruhiro and the party fought back to the best of their ability. They were strange foes. They were probably hairy creatures, and they didn't use their voices, bite, or claw at them. They just rammed into them. They weren't heavy blows, and were kind of soft. It was less like a tackle, and more like they were pushing them, maybe? It wasn't that hard to dodge, or to knock them away, to be honest. But their opponents didn't give up. They came one after another.

Finally, Momohina lost her patience. "Nyahahh! Delm, hel, en, balk, zel, arve!"

Her Blast spell exploded. The blast revealed their enemies' identity.

Hair. They were hair. Hair. That was all you could call them. There were hair monsters here, there, and everywhere.

The hair monsters scattered like the tide going out, but they soon rushed in again. Even when Momohina let off another Blast, they eventually came again, and there was no way to handle them.

Haruhiro tried grabbing one and stabbing it with his dagger, but stab as he might, he didn't feel like he was hitting anything but hair. It was revolting to see the hair he cut off squirming, too.

The hair monsters pressed in on them again and again until dawn came. In the early morning, during their final attack, as the hair monsters fled, Haruhiro realized something. He had thought each of them was different. However, he spotted a phenomenon where one fleeing hair would attach to another, and then that hair monster to yet another. Ultimately, each of the wriggling hairs scattered on the ground gathered up, tangled together, and ran away from the party...

Which meant? What did it mean? While wracking his brain over it, he felt a disconcerting hypothesis coming to mind. It was time to drop it.

Because of the hair, Haruhiro hadn't gotten a wink of sleep, but he was going to have to get to the dragons' nest, return the egg, and get out of here already. The party rushed onward. It was painful enough that he was weirdly high strung, but so what? Think about it. Was anything not painful? Yeah, maybe. But weren't those things few and far between? Didn't he spend more time suffering than not? Besides, there were different types of pain. This was the type he could manage somehow. He didn't feel like he couldn't get through it.

In the morning, three dragons took flight. What was happening to Roronea? Now wasn't the time to think about that.

In the morning, Yume stepped on a pure white snake that was over ten meters long, and almost got swallowed whole. Kuzaku fell from a tree, making the monkeys all laugh at him, and got chased around by a creature that was like a giant hermit crab. Shihoru fainted, and Kuzaku threw his back out carrying her, so Merry had to heal him. Other than that, nothing much happened.

In the afternoon, they were attacked by a swarm of meter-long butterflies, or moths, or something. They tried to climb a tree, but it was actually a mass of green cockroach-like insects. Then, when they were running away from them in a panic, Haruhiro, Kuzaku, and Yume fell down a fissure-like hole where bugs swarmed in, and they ended up in real trouble.

It was a situation that forced Haruhiro to think that the day he could laugh it off saying, *It never occurred to me I'd rather have a proper bath than be bathed in insects before, ha ha ha,* was never going to come.

They encountered a creature that shot spear-like projectiles from its mouth, and were shocked to see it take out a monkey in the treetops. Then, as might be expected, they were attacked themselves and forced to fight it. Nothing good happened the whole day.

Even so, they managed to take little breaks here and there, and were careful not to get totally exhausted. They were used to traveling, after all. They didn't forget the importance of rest.

Before dusk, they spotted the dragons returning to the nest. They looked pretty big. That surely meant the nest was close. They didn't know if it was exceptionally close, but they were getting closer.

It felt like the hair monsters might come again, so they kept cautiously moving forward even once the sun went down. Naturally, that necessitated lighting a lamp. They covered it, and did their best to only light the area around their feet. But after some time, they no longer needed the light. An incredible number of bugs that shone like fireflies started flying around.

Thinking, *They're bugs, right?* Haruhiro tried catching one, and it vanished, light and all.

"It's a supernatural phenomenon, huuuuh?" Momohina grinned. "Heh heh heh!"

Momohina was laughing, but Kuzaku and Shihoru looked seriously freaked out. The way the countless flickering pale blue lights dimly lit the green forest made for a mysterious and beautiful scene. It was so beautiful that it gave you goosebumps, and there was something frightening about it.

What were those lights? Were they a natural phenomenon? Or supernatural like Momohina'd suggested? Were they disembodied souls? That sort of thought crossed his mind. The lights were gathering into human-like shapes, after all.

Weren't the human-like figures kind of, like, following them? Weren't they increasing in number? Was he just imagining that? No, right?

"Th-th-th-this is s-s-s-s-somewhat disconcerting, d-d-don't you think?" It was a little surprising that Setora was scared.

If he asked if she was scared, she'd probably deny it, but her knees were shaking, so he figured she was frightened. Because of that, she was unsteady on her feet, and there were several times when she almost tripped.

"Here, it's dangerous." Merry tried to support her, but Setora refused.

"M-m-mind your own business." She immediately tripped, and Merry pulled her to her feet. From there on, Setora didn't refuse help, and they walked leaning on each other for support.

When the party stopped to rest, the masses of light stopped, too. When they began moving forward, the masses of light always came with them. What were those things…?

When the night came to an end, the countless lights and the masses of light vanished in an instant, as if they had never been there.

Looking around, the party was shocked and amazed.

The forest was no longer green. It was orange. What was more, it continued to change. As they walked on, and the sun rose higher and brighter, the trees, the ground, and everything but the clear blue sky turned yellow.

It was truly yellow. Was this possible? After the incident with the lights the night before, it felt like they'd wandered into another world.

Wait, did we die at some point, maybe? Is this not just another world, but the world after death? Haruhiro wondered.

From between the yellow trees, they spotted a greenish yellow—or a yellow-green—mountain, and they witnessed three dragons taking off from there one after another. That convinced Haruhiro they were still alive.

"Hold on," he said, stopping.

The nest. The dragons' nest was on top of that yellow-green mountain. They were already in the caldera on top of a mountain, but there was another mountain here. It was yellow-green, too. It was really pretty, though. It made them realize all over again what an unknown frontier this was. They had no idea what else might be waiting for them.

There had to be stuff even more incredible than what they'd seen. There couldn't not be. It would be weird. Crazy.

But they went on and on, and nothing happened. Incredibly, they reached Yellow-Green Mountain around noon. (It was a yellow-green mountain, so they called it Yellow-Green Mountain.)

Eyeballing it, it looked to be around maybe four hundred meters high. It was small for a mountain. The slope wasn't steep, either. They could climb a mountain like this in about two hours. If there were no accidents, that was. It was still noon, so they could climb there and back by evening. The dragons wouldn't come back and run into them while they were in the nest. Hopefully...

They considered playing it safe, staying the night here, and heading for the mountain the next morning once the dragons took off. However, if it took an extra day, there would be that many more casualties.

The dragons might not stop their destruction even once the egg was returned to the nest, but, well, they'd cross that bridge if they came to it. They had come this far, after all. They'd do what they could as soon as possible. That was all there was to it.

The ascent of Yellow-Green Mountain went smoothly. Looking out from up high, the view was nothing short of breathtaking. Here, with Yellow-Green Mountain as the center, the yellow trees spread out looking like a field of flowers in full bloom, and they were surrounded by a forest so brilliantly green, it seemed unreal.

The runarukas referred to this entire area as the dragons' nest. Even seeing such a mysterious and wonderful sight made the trip here worth it. That said, Haruhiro never wanted to come back, and he wanted to get their task done quickly so they could go home. That didn't mean they rushed, but it was an easy mountain to climb, so they ascended the summit in half the expected time, and they found the nest in no time, too.

The entrance to the nest, to be precise.

There was a hole open in the peak of Yellow-Green Mountain. It had to be large enough for dragons to come out of, so it was probably about forty meters across. It was a slightly warped, round, vertical shaft. Peering in, they could see what looked like the bottom down below.

Not clearly. It was pretty deep. Easily over a hundred meters.

They couldn't descend from here. It wasn't just a sheer cliff; there were places where it was worse than just being straight down. They would have to fall to reach the bottom. Of course, if they did that, they would die.

Shihoru sat down, exhausted. "What...now..." she said in a voice that sounded ready to give out.

"Hmm..." Kuzaku crossed his arms and groaned.

Setora took a breath, then shook her head. Kiichi was at her feet, batting his eyes.

Merry had a difficult look on her face, and Haruhiro nearly couldn't stop looking at her, but he hurriedly turned away. Yume stood shoulder-to-shoulder with Momohina at the precipice, looking down into bottom of the hole.

"There's another way," Haruhiro said, then nodded. There couldn't not be. Absolutely, there was one. "We're overlooking it. Or more like we've never looked for it to begin with. Somewhere on the mountain slope, there's a side path leading into the nest. Now we just have to find it."

There was no guarantee they could pass through that side path unharmed, and not only would they have trouble on the way back, but it was so dangerous that he didn't want to think about it. But he deliberately ignored all of that. They would overcome things one at a time, moving forward step by step. That was how they'd done it all this time. They'd do it here, too.

Haruhiro would have liked to split up, but if they split into groups, they would have no way to contact each other, and there was the risk that some would wander astray. So they would fundamentally move as a group, spreading out to search as wide an area as they could manage without losing sight of one another.

Even for a little mountain like this one, it would take a long time to search every nook and cranny of it. It would have been nice to have some idea where to look. If the bottom of the nest hole was more than a hundred meters down, the side path leading to it couldn't be that high up. It was a little hard to imagine it would be near the base, either.

First they'd do a thorough search of the middle area. In times like this, Kiichi the gray nyaa often proved more useful than any human. They let Kiichi act on his own, trusting that he'd tell them if anything looked like what they were after.

With that sorted out, as they were about to descend from the summit to get to work, there was a cute, but still quite loud cry that echoed through the area.

Pigyahhhhhh!

Haruhiro turned his eyes towards the nest hole. He didn't want to look, but he couldn't not, so he did.

Flapping its wings, it appeared from inside the nest hole. In many ways, *No way,* was his honest response.

Why was it here? Three of them had flown off, right? Well, even if they knew there were multiple dragons, no one had known the exact number there were. It just meant there were actually four.

Hold on, it was small. Even with its wings spread wide, it might only have a span of four, five meters. That was still large, but compared to the dragons repeatedly attacking Roronea, he couldn't help but think, *It's tiny!*

Its head seemed weirdly big, too. Like it had a child-sized body. Its flying was kind of awkward, too. It was beating its wings as hard as it could, but its ascent was slow. That said, the small emerald dragon was already looking down at Haruhiro and the party from a height of twenty, thirty meters.

"Ahh... Ahh! Ahhhhhhhhhhhhh!!" Kuzaku started scream-ing too late.

"Haruhiro-kun?!" Shihoru cried.

"Haru?!"

"Haru!"

"Haru-kun?!"

His comrades called his name one after another.

No, don't ask me what to do.

He wanted to turn to Momohina for orders, but Haruhiro had his pride as a leader. Or not. He didn't have much. But the grim fact was that he was their leader.

What now? Like, even if it was small, it was a dragon. It was flying, too. That, and if they fought it, even if they were lucky enough to win, what then? That had to be a young dragon. They had come here to return the egg and appease the dragons' anger, so killing a young dragon was clearly not okay. There was no choice to be made. They had only one option.

"Run...! Split up!"

They all rushed down Yellow-Green Mountain as one. He'd said to split up, but Haruhiro followed behind Shihoru. Everyone else would be fine. Probably.

Turning back, the young dragon cried, *Pigyahhhhhhhhhhhhh!* It didn't attack. The young dragon was still in about the same spot as before. It made Haruhiro want to slow his pace, but no.

The young dragon continued crying, *Pigyahhhhhh, pigyahh-hhhh!* It cried like crazy. That voice would reach a long distance. Could it be? Just maybe, was it calling them? Was it trying to call back the three dragons? Even if it was, how long would it take them to fly here?

It was much faster to descend than to climb. Haruhiro and Shihoru brought up the rear, but they probably still took less than an hour to get down the mountain.

The young dragon was still repeating its cry of, *Pigyahh, pigyahh!*

Right before they dove into the yellow forest, Haruhiro saw dragons flying in from the south. Once they were in the forest, trees obstructed the view, so he couldn't confirm it. They had been distant specks, but he was sure they'd been the dragons. Would it be best to hide somewhere? Or did they need to run much, much farther? He had to decide. Which was better? Even if they were going to hide, would there conveniently be a place for them to do it around here? Even if they were to keep running, everyone was winded. This was what having no way out felt like.

In the end, there was a tremendous roar as one dragon flew straight over the party.

Gyohhhhhhhhhhhhhhhhhhhhhhhhhhhhhn!

It was still above the treetops, but it still felt as if it had grazed the tops of their heads.

"It's coming!" someone shouted.

Shihoru wasn't moving. Had her legs gone numb with fear? Haruhiro put an arm around Shihoru and ran. He was running, but what would that do?

It was coming. Again. For real this time. From the opposite direction, behind them. Most likely, it had changed directions, then done a rapid dive.

Haruhiro pushed Shihoru forward diagonally, then turned to face it. He had thought it was coming for him, but not that it was this close. It was at close range. The dragon mowed down trees as it attempted to land. It was right in front of his nose. A cloud of dust rose up, and he was blown away. Haruhiro spun once, then twice. *Oh, no, it's going to step on me!* he thought, but he didn't remember why. Whatever the case, Haruhiro was clinging to the dragon. Its rear leg, apparently. The right one, huh?

The dragon roared, *Agyoooooooooooooon!* and thrashed around. It would shake him off in no time.

He didn't particularly want to cling to a dragon, but he was sure he'd die in a second if he were to let go. Haruhiro instinctively drew his dagger with the flame-like blade and stabbed the polished metal into the dragon's scales. An ordinary sword might not have stabbed through. The flame dagger was no ordinary blade. It slid in deep. He couldn't pull it free, either.

The dragon was still stamping its feet and jumping. Haruhiro held the hilt of his flame dagger tight with his left hand, then drew his other dagger with his right hand.

This other dagger was also a product of the dwarf hole. It could do this. In theory. He stabbed.

Good, he thought. It went in. That was when it happened.

Uwah!

The dragon was bending its legs, sort of like it would do before a big jump—

Wait, is it about to fly? Should I let go?

By the time he thought that, it was too late.

The moment the dragon jumped, he felt a floating sensation. Fast. It was going damn fast. It happened in an instant.

He was already in the air. Way above the trees. It was a clear difference from that young dragon. The power it had to ascend by beating its wings was not to be underestimated.

"Wahhhhhhhhhhhhhhhhhhhhhhhhhhhhhhhhhhhhhhhhhh..." Haruhiro screamed despite himself.

The thought to look for his comrades occurred to him, but it was a little impossible. He was up in the sky, after all.

Flying, too.

Was he a hundred meters up by now? More, maybe?

It looked like the dragon kept its legs fixed in a slightly bent position while flying. Maybe if it moved too much while flying, that threw off its balance.

Thanks to that, as long as Haruhiro kept a firm grip on the flame dagger, it didn't look like he'd fall. Right. For as long he was able to hang on. But that was pretty hard to do.

When he'd stabbed the flame dagger and normal dagger through the dragon's scales, he'd given up on clinging to the dragon's leg. Unlike a human leg, the dragon's leg was as thick as a big tree trunk, so he couldn't have clung to it for that long to begin with. Therefore, his left and right hands' grip on the flame dagger and normal dagger were his only hope.

Haruhiro felt the wind on basically his whole body. The wind force was intense. He was going to be sent flying, seriously. It was a mystery to him how he hadn't been yet. Well, he knew if he was knocked off, it'd be the end of him, so he was holding on for dear life.

High. It was so high up. How many hundreds of meters were they up now? Was it thousands? More? Incredible. He could see the whole of Emerald Island. He could see the other islands, too. This was on a whole different level from just being scary. Though, that said, it was scary, too. How long would his grip last? He wasn't sure.

Each time the dragon moved its wings, he was tossed around. He felt like his whole body was being torn up. Not just his physical body, but his very existence.

Eventually the dragon began descending and ascending. It was too much. He really couldn't take it anymore. He couldn't rouse himself to action. He could only cry that he couldn't do it, he was at his limit, and hang in there.

Then the dragon started whipping around and doing horizontal and vertical spins.

Are you trying to kill me? Enough already. Please. Stop it, he silently begged, but could still only hold on.

Suddenly, he lost his grip on the flame dagger with his left hand. *It's over,* he resigned himself. *This is the end. I'm absolutely finished.*

However, when the dragon did a turn after that, his body swung majorly. He stretched his left hand out using the momentum from that, and he managed to reach the hilt of the flame dagger.

He was just a little relieved, but at the same time felt fed up. What, it wasn't over yet? If it was going to end, it should've just ended. That would've been easier. He'd had enough.

Even when his comrades flashed though his mind, he couldn't think, *I'll try again.* Well, why was he hanging on by the skin of his teeth, then? Wasn't this enough? He'd done what he could. More than anyone could have expected. If it ended here, he'd have no regrets.

Really?

He decided to stop thinking about it. Or rather, he stopped being able to think anymore.

He occasionally let out screams like, *Wahh,* or, *Ohhh,* or, *Aargh.*

There were several occasions where his left hand or his right was separated from a dagger's hilt. How did he recover? He had no clue. The next thing he knew, both hands were on their respective hilts.

The sea was beautiful.

So blue.

At some point, they had come out over the sea.

The dragon's wings were still spread, its body tilted on a slight angle, and it was circling gently. It seemed to be slowly descending.

That was...

A town?

There was only one town on the island. The dragon was heading from the sea towards Roronea.

It flew over the ruined piers and wharves. There was hardly any trace left of the warehouses. Beyond them was the commercial district. That had been heavily damaged, too, and the former marketplace was nothing but scrap and rubble.

The dragon beat its wings. Its speed dropped instantly, and Haruhiro's body was lifted up. He nearly lost his grip on his daggers' hilts—or rather, he wanted to let go of them, but he just couldn't. His fingers, his hands, his arms... none of them would listen to him.

The impact of landing was intense. His whole body was shaken harder than ever, and he wondered if his head might pop off.

Haruhiro was currently clinging to the flame dagger and normal dagger, which were thrust into the dragon's leg, and hanging down from there. He was conscious of his current state, but it didn't feel real.

Feelings. Yes. His senses weren't there. He was cold. His whole body. It was like he was frozen.

The dragon shuddered a little, and let out a short, low vocalization. *Woh!*

He could tell it was trying to say something. Haruhiro nodded, breathing repeatedly. Eventually, he returned to something approaching body temperature.

They moved. His fingers. His hands. His arms. His legs, too. He could move them.

"...Hold on."

Haruhiro wrapped both his legs around the dragon's leg, pulling both the flame dagger and normal dagger free with all his might. They hadn't come out all this time, but now they actually pulled free.

Haruhiro dropped to the ground with the flame dagger and normal dagger. He tried to land gracefully, but he couldn't quite manage it, so he hit himself in a few places and it hurt. But he was alive... Right? *Am I alive?* he wondered.

He couldn't be confident. He looked around. This was probably the area that had once been Roronea's market. There should have been tens of stalls and shops here, maybe more, and the remains of them were scattered around.

Why was he here? He'd been at the dragons' nest not long ago. This was weird. It didn't make sense.

Haruhiro got up. He hurt all over. Dragging his leg, he staggered on.

When he suddenly turned back, the dragon had raised its head and was looking at him.

Man, it was big. Seriously.

The dragon's mouth was closed. Its nostrils flared as it breathed in and out, and the dragon's scales sparkled in time with those subtle motions. Its yellow eyes were more incredible than its scales. They were the essence of light itself. How could such a creature exist?

It struck Haruhiro's heart. A feeling of awe, you could say.

It's no good. No way. Something like this. This incredible creature. You can't do something that would anger it.

Haruhiro pulled the egg from his bag and, backing away, he knelt down and placed it gently on the ground.

"Sorry. We wanted to return this. We went to give it back."

The dragon tilted its head for just a moment, then blinked.

What did it feel? What was it thinking? He didn't have a clue. But though it probably thought and felt completely differently from how a human did, the dragon was definitely feeling something, and probably thinking, too.

The dragon stretched its neck out. Was this where Haruhiro was going to get eaten now? If it was, there was nothing he could do. Not at this distance. He couldn't run away. Whether Haruhiro lived or died was up to the dragon. There were things he couldn't do anything about. Haruhiro took a deep breath and stayed put.

The dragon gripped the egg in its jaws. It tilted its head back.

With the egg still in its mouth, it let out a low voice. *Ohh, wao, ohh!*

Haruhiro stood up. The dragon beat its wings two, three times, and took off.

Buffeted by the wind, Haruhiro fell on his backside. From there, he looked up at the dragon. It climbed and climbed.

Haruhiro fell back, looking straight up. The dragon circled Roronea once, then went off into the distance. Then, finally, he lost sight of it.

Haruhiro whispered to himself, "I'm tired..."

Grimgar
of
Fantasy and Ash

SINCE THEN, Roronea hadn't been attacked.

Momohina, Kuzaku, and the rest of the party returned four days later. His comrades had been praying for Haruhiro's safety, no doubt, but they must have feared the worst. They were all overjoyed and mobbed him. There were a whole lot of tears. Haruhiro's eyes got a little misty, too.

The restoration of Roronea was proceeding at an incredible pace. The last of the piers and wharves had actually been wiped out while the party were going to the dragons' nest, but by the time Kuzaku and the others returned, there were two temporary piers in a somewhat usable state.

Transportation using ships with barges had been restarted before then, and little by little, supplies had begun to enter Roronea. The dead were mourned, and buildings were rebuilt here and there.

The day after they were reunited, the party went to the temporary No. 1 Pier and boarded the *Mantis-go,* captained by Ginzy.

There were a number of other ships trying to leave port, but the loading of cargo and crew had already been completed for the most part. Despite that, not just the temporary No. 1 Pier but the No. 2 Pier beside it were packed with people, people, and more people.

"Hero of Roronea!"

"Dragon Rider!"

"Hey, rich man!"

"Spend some of it before you go, ya cheapskate!"

"Ya did well! I'm mildly impressed!"

"Haruhirooo! I'll never forget you guys! Don't you ever come back!"

"Come back sometime and play, you damn hero!"

"You don't need to come back, damn it! Thanks, Dragon Rider!"

Young and old, men and women of every race shouted whatever they wanted, thrusting fists into the air and jumping up and down. Looking at them from the side of the ship, it was hard to think they were talking about him.

Kuzaku poked him in the shoulder. "Why don't you wave?"

Even as he thought, *What're you grinning for?* Haruhiro waved to the people half out of desperation.

The crowd roared when he did, but what was he supposed to think about this, really? It felt like it was happening to someone else, and he couldn't even feel embarrassed by it.

"Well, the fact of the matter is, you saved the lot of them. I would say that merits being called a hero, wouldn't you?" Setora had an unpleasantly serious look on her face.

Nyaoh, Kiichi meowed from down at Setora's feet.

A hero, huh? Haruhiro scratched his head at the thought of it.

Setora murmured, "Dragon Rider," and then burst out laughing.

"You're laughing," Haruhiro muttered.

"I mean, it's not as if you actually rode the dragon."

That was true. Haruhiro had never ridden a dragon. He clung to the dragon like some piece of trash that had gotten tangled on it, and managed to fly from the dragons' nest to Roronea.

There were some people still staying in Roronea's marketplace because it was dangerous no matter where they went, and they had coincidentally witnessed Haruhiro returning the egg to the dragon. Yet it was unlikely anyone had witnessed exactly how the dragon had carried Haruhiro there. That being the case, the story was quickly embellished, warped, and expanded, to the point that he had come riding in on the dragon's back, earning him the nickname Dragon Rider. He found it a bit embarrassing.

"From a Goblin Slayer to a Dragon Rider..." Shihoru was giggling.

"Hey, not you, too, Shihoru," he protested.

"Sorry. But I don't think you can avoid being the talk of the town..."

"He's a hero, after all, right?" Setora looked ready to burst out in a fit of laughter at any moment.

How am I supposed to be a hero? Give me a break.

"Well, we made a solid profit, though." Kuzaku slapped the oddly impressive bag he had slung over his shoulder. "That's thanks to you, Haruhiro. You're our hero, too."

The bag was full of platinum coins. Each one was worth ten gold coins. Gold coins were one thing, but unless someone was a merchant with a lot of turnover or a wealthy individual with considerable assets, a person would almost never see platinum coins.

Even if the story about the dragon's egg being worth five thousand gold was nonsense, the work they'd be doing had to be worth at least a thousand.

Before going to return the egg, he'd tried that line on Giancarlo, who had blown him off with , *Don't be stupid!* But after negotiating, they'd settled on the amount of five hundred gold coins.

That was five hundred gold. It was still a dizzying amount of wealth.

Incidentally, the bag Kuzaku was carrying had one hundred platinum coins, which each weighed thirty grams. In other words, a thousand gold.

Giancarlo was looking vacantly up at the *Mantis-go* from the temporary No. 1 Pier. It must have been the continuous days of intense work. He looked pretty sleepy.

When the people of Roronea spoke of Haruhiro's great deed, the story of how the K&K Pirate Company had rewarded him a thousand gold for his work always came with it. That was a rumor that Giancarlo and Jimmy, who was now standing next to him with one hand raised, had actively worked to spread.

There were some who were impressed by the K&K Pirate Company's largesse, while others snapped, saying, *If they have all that money, they should be giving it to me.* Either way, an unimpressive adventurer—or volunteer soldier, actually, but a total unknown either way—had made a fortune in no time flat. It was what might be called the Roronean Dream.

Figuring a thousand gold would be twice as impactful as five hundred, Giancarlo and Jimmy had gone all-out on the reward. In fact, Roronea was in a fever now.

For the present at least, this fever would give an extra push to the reconstruction of Roronea. Haruhiro felt inconvenienced as the one who had to carry the burden of a manufactured legend, but a thousand gold was a lot. Converted to the silver they actually used in their daily lives, it was a hundred thousand coins. In copper, it was ten million. Unbelievable.

"Still, I'm glad." Merry narrowed her eyes, looking off into the distance somewhere.

Looking at Merry's smile, Haruhiro was able to honestly admit, *Well, I guess I'm glad, too.* A lot had happened, but now they could move on.

Ginzy pretentiously ordered, "Hoist the sails!" and the *Mantis-go's* sails were hoisted.

Then he signaled for them to "Weigh anchor!" and the crew went about weighing anchor.

The people crowded on the pier whirled their coats or handkerchiefs above their heads, going, *Yo ho, yo ho!* and making a scene.

"Huh?" Haruhiro looked around the area.

"Huh? What's up?" Kuzaku asked him, but he just gave a vague nod as he looked here and there.

What's this, what's this?

"Ah..." Shihoru gulped.

"Wait!" Merry leaned out over the said of the ship.

"Hm?" Setora put her hand on the gunwale. "Oh..."

Kiichi jumped onto the gunwale meowing, *Nyaoh.*

The *Mantis-go* was already moving.

"Yume?!" Haruhiro pushed in between Merry and Setora, looking intently at the temporary No. 1 Pier.

Giancarlo was there, Jimmy was there. Then there was Momohina, with a false mustache, a stern look on her face, and her arms crossed. Finally, beside her was Yume, waving a cloth scrap around and shouting, "Yo ho, yo ho!"

"No, not 'yo ho'—Huh? Why?! Yume?! Since when..."

"She was here just a moment ago...wasn't she?" Merry said, seeming less than confident.

"Hey, what are you playing at?!" Setora shouted.

Yume burst into a full-faced grin. "Ahh! Hey, listen! Yume, she's havin' Momohina train her, 'cause she's decided to be a real kung-fulier!"

"Why?!" Shihoru asked, her voice going shrill.

Yeah. Why? This was coming out of nowhere. It made no sense.

Maybe because it was so surprising, Shihoru sounded ready to cry.

"Well, you know! Yume just couldn't bring herself to say it!" Yume was tearing up.

There was a clutching in Haruhiro's chest, and he came back to his senses.

Yume had kind of never made much sense to begin with. If he were to describe her with one word, it'd be "ditzy." She wasn't a boring, ordinary person like Haruhiro, who tended to ingratiate himself to people, read social cues, compromise, and pick his words so the other party members could understand him.

Yume had her own thoughts and feelings, and a unique way of expressing them. That was why, honestly, Haruhiro never sufficiently understood exactly what Yume was feeling or thinking.

He'd thought that was just how she was. That he didn't really need to understand. It'd probably be fine.

They'd gotten by like this all along. Everyone loved Yume, and they wanted her to stay that same Yume forever. Even if they didn't say a word, Yume would be Yume, and she'd stay with them as if that were a given. He'd believed that without a shred of doubt. The truth was that Yume probably had worries of her own, and hopes for something, and might even have her own secret ambitions, but he'd never thought about that.

"Sorry, everyone! Yume wants to get stronger! She's been thinkin' she wants to get way, way stronger! If she's with Momohina-chan, it feels like she can make Yume stronger! We'll meet back up in Alterna, half a year from now! By that time, Yume, she's gonna get realllll strong!"

Now that she mentioned it, on their first day in Roronea, Yume had been asking Momohina if she could get stronger. He had the feeling Momohina had answered that Yume might be on the right track already, and if she trained her for three, four months, she'd be an honest to goodness kung-fulier or something like that.

257

But, really, she wanted to get stronger? Haruhiro couldn't say that was stupid, or that she didn't have to get stronger. This was what Yume had wished for, what she had chosen. It might be coming out of nowhere, but that was a very Yume thing to do.

"Half a year...!" Haruhiro sniffled. He forced a smile. He took a deep breath. "We'll be waiting! Half a year from now, in Alterna!"

"Yep!" Momohina slapped Yume on the back as hard as she could. "Leave her to meeee! I'll raise Yumeyume to be a real honest to goodness kung-fulieeeer! Indeeeed!"

"Seriously...?" Kuzaku collapsed to the deck and hung his head.

Shihoru had no words, just waving her hand.

Setora and Kiichi were dumbfounded.

Merry put an arm around Shihoru's shoulder.

The *Mantis-go* picked up speed.

Thus was a legend born, and for months and years to come, it would continue to be handed down.

HOW WAS IT? Volume 12 of *Grimgar of Fantasy and Ash*?

As announced in advance, I think it was a cheery, fun, fluffy adventure story.

This doesn't only apply to *Grimgar,* but when writing novels, it is common for me to not decide on the minute details of what is going to happen, who is going to do what, and why in advance. Sometimes, at least; there are also times when I plan everything out in detail before I start writing. However, when I do that, it tends not to go well. I can make progress writing, but I can't get in the mood, and I have to come up with various ways to make writing fun.

You can write novels however you like, and I love them for that freedom, but I have just one rule that I follow.

I want, more than anything, for people to enjoy the novels that I write. If I'm not having fun writing a novel, it's probably boring, so I try to enjoy writing. I won't let a manuscript I didn't enjoy writing out into the world.

If I feel like, *This is no fun,* I decide to stop writing at that point.

There are times I don't realize it while writing, or I notice I've been lying to myself that it's fun, or I'm under time pressure and forget to have fun as I write. If I reread it and think, *Yeah, I wasn't having fun here,* I immediately throw it out.

When I go, *This happens, then this, and it turns out like this,* deciding all the details before I write, I'm often unable to have fun.

Still, that said, if I don't decide on anything, I have no idea where the story is headed, and I can't even get started writing.

The point at which I've planned enough and can figure out the rest is something that I've more or less learned from experience.

However, when something occurs to me, I try testing to see whether I should decide more in advance. Can I assemble a more complex story? Or if I reduce the number of things I decide in advance by one or two, what will happen?

For Volume 12, I chose the key points of the first half in advance, or the first third of the story, and then left the rest to the flow of things.

What will I do next time? I have a number of ideas. Which will I choose? I'm looking forward to finding out.

To my editor, Harada-san, to Eiri Shirai-san, to the designers of KOMEWORKS among others, to everyone involved in production and sales of this book, and finally to all of you people now holding this book, I offer my heartfelt appreciation and all of my love. Now, I lay down my pen for today.

I hope we will meet again.

—Ao Jyumonji

Grimgar of Fantasy and Ash

Experience these great light novel titles from Seven Seas Entertainment